THE GOLDFISH BOWL

THE GOLDFISH BOWL

A NOVEL

by

LAURENCE GOUGH

LONDON

VICTOR GOLLANCZ LTD

1987

First published in Great Britain 1987
by Victor Gollancz Ltd,
14 Henrietta Street, London WC2E 8QJ

British Library Cataloguing in Publication Data
Gough, Laurence
  The goldfish bowl.
  I. Title
  813′ .54[F]   PR9199.3.G65/

  ISBN 0–575–03935–3

Typeset at The Spartan Press Ltd,
Lymington, Hants
and printed in Great Britain by
St Edmundsbury Press Ltd, Bury St Edmunds, Suffolk

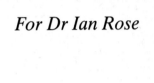

For Dr Ian Rose

I

THE SNIPER LIVED in a corner apartment on the twelfth floor of an anonymous grey highrise in the middle of the city's West End. From the balcony it was possible to glimpse a narrow wedge of the dark, choppy waters of English Bay, the lights of the downtown core, and, almost directly below, the gaudy stained-glass figures in the windows of St Paul's.

In front of the church stood a Japanese plum, its pink buds charred black by the incandescent streetlight on the corner. In the sparse shadow of the tree a prostitute smoked a cigarette down to the filter, idly flicked the butt into the gutter.

The air was cold and damp, heavy with the threat of rain. The hooker glanced up, looking for stars, but the lights of the surrounding buildings dominated the night sky and all she saw was the vague outline of a man peering down at her from a narrow slab of balcony made even smaller by the distance between them.

The man, looking down, saw the hooker lean back and then wave up at him. He immediately turned his back to her, and disappeared from view.

Inside, the apartment was warm, spotlessly clean, and smelled faintly of latex paint and of varnish from the freshly sanded floors.

There was very little in the way of furniture. A bright orange plastic basket-chair and a rough pine table with folding steel legs stood directly beneath the ceiling fixture, and a foam-rubber slab and rumpled blue and green plaid sleeping bag lay against one of the bare white walls. But otherwise, the apartment was empty.

A Winchester .460 Magnum rifle equipped with a Redfield variable-power scope lay diagonally across one end of the pine table. The blued metal and rich burled walnut of the stock gleamed under the light cast from a chrome-plated goose-neck

7

lamp. Next to the Winchester stood a small can of cleaning fluid, a jointed brass cleaning-rod, and a litter of cloth patches stained yellow with machine oil.

The sniper sat in the orange plastic chair, hunched over a Lyman 'All American' turret press. His hands were large and strong. The thick blunt fingers, nails carefully painted with a glossy red polish, moved with precision and grace as he assembled the shiny brass cartridges, primers, powder and fat 500-grain copper-jacketed slugs. Pulling firmly on the handle of the Lyman, he forced lead into brass and, all in one easy motion, crimped the fully assembled bullet.

Behind him, in the kitchenette, an open bottle of Scotch stood on the counter next to a stack of paper cups and half a loaf of crumbly French bread. Next to the bread was a portable radio, and from the tiny speaker Willie Nelson sung softly and persuasively of love. The sniper hummed along for a few bars, and then, concentrating on his task, lost track of the tune. The results of many weeks of intense labour were now only a few hours away. He had worked hard, fussed interminably over every last detail, no matter how small or insignificant. And now, finally, he was sure he had done everything he could to ensure that his plan would be successful. Still, he was more than a little nervous. Luck was the one factor that no amount of planning could eliminate. If luck wasn't on his side tonight, all his careful plans would be for nothing.

A drop of sweat trickled down his cheek, followed the line of his jaw to his chin and then dropped between his thighs and splattered in miniscule beads on the gleaming hardwood floor. The sniper wiped his face with the back of his hand. He inserted the freshly-made bullet into one of the Winchester's spare magazines, pushed away from the table and moved purposefully towards the bottle of Scotch.

On the radio, Willie had finished and Johnny Cash was singing in a voice like a rasp about the tedium of life behind bars. The sniper turned the volume down just a little. He got ice from the fridge and poured an inch of Scotch into one of the paper cups, screwed the cap back on the bottle. He carried his drink from the kitchen to the sliding glass door fronting the balcony, and went outside. The rain had stopped for a little while but now it had begun again. The prostitute had vanished.

The sniper was standing in the middle of one of the most densely populated square miles in all of North America. He was surrounded on all sides by tens of thousands of people. And yet he felt completely alone.

It was a nice feeling.

He downed the Scotch and, as the ice rattled against his teeth, decided to pour himself a refill. But just one, only the one. He had a very demanding and dangerous night ahead of him, and if he hoped to get through it in one piece he was going to have to stay stone-cold sober.

Alice Palm sat at the head of the oak gate-leg table her mother had forcibly wedged into the tiny eating nook, which from then on had always, with no undercurrent of irony, been referred to as the dining room. The remains of a baked potato and a congealing lamb chop lay in front of Alice on a pink and white Spode plate. She used her knife and fork to separate delicately a last sliver of meat from the bone, chewed unhurriedly, and swallowed. Putting the utensils down side by side on the plate, she patted her lips with a napkin of brilliant white linen.

Alice lived in apartment 104 of The Berkely, a squat building three storeys high, with a red-brick façade marred by recently installed aluminium windows. She had shared the apartment with her mother for almost thirty years, lived there alone for the past decade. The Berkely was ideally situated. It was only a fifteen-minute bus ride from the downtown office where she worked as a secretary, only a short walk from the beaches and the thousand green acres of Stanley Park, and less than two blocks from her church, St Paul's.

After her mother died, Alice had toyed with the idea of moving, but had eventually and inevitably decided against it. She felt comfortable with the old apartment, the dim, high-ceilinged rooms, the faded and ornately patterned wallpaper, the familiar sights and sounds and smells of the neighbourhood.

Alice stood up, collected the dishes and stacked them in her antiquated sink. Then she crossed the narrow hallway to the bathroom and ran the water full blast into the huge, claw-footed enamel tub. As the tub filled with water and the bathroom filled with steam, Alice washed and dried the dinner dishes and put them away in the small leaded glass cabinets above the countertop of square yellow tiles.

By the time she'd finished with the dishes, the tub was nearly full. She turned off the taps, tested the temperature of the water, and mixed in a packet of lilac bath gel. The room filled with the delicate scent of flowers. She undressed and stepped gingerly into the tub.

An hour later and much refreshed, she sat in front of the bow-front dresser mirror in her bedroom. Her hair was wrapped in a thick pink towel, and there were still a few drops of lilac-scented water scattered across her shoulders and the smooth white skin of her back. Except for a pair of black lace panties she was naked. Behind her, a Dici bra, freshly pressed blouse, pale green V-neck sweater and dark green pleated skirt lay folded across the wooden footboard of her double bed.

She leaned a little closer to the mirror, her breasts swaying, and carefully examined her face. There appeared to be neither more nor fewer lines than had existed a week ago. She smiled softly, forgiving herself her small vanities, and then began to apply the makeup that was still more of a celebration than a necessity. A touch of powder to accent her cheekbones, a trace of liner around her pale green eyes. Lipstick that was darker and glossier than she'd ever have dared wear to work, and that somehow made her mouth seem wider and vaguely carnal.

Alice pouted into the mirror, licked her lips with the tip of her tongue, took the weight of her breasts in her hands. Watching the reflected nipples distend, she pressed her thighs together and tried to imagine the evening that lay ahead.

It was Friday night, and, as usual, Alice Palm was going out on the town.

Of all the amenities afforded by his new apartment, the one the sniper appreciated the most was the secured underground parking. The stolen bright yellow Honda Civic with the crumpled right rear fender was exactly as he had left it, in one of the half-dozen parking spots reserved for tenants' guests. He opened the driver's door, laid the soft leather gun case across the back seat, and climbed awkwardly behind the wheel. Leaning forward, he reached under the dashboard and crossed the red and blue ignition wires. The little four-cylinder engine caught immediately.

While the engine warmed, the sniper examined himself in the rearview mirror. Like Alice, he had dressed carefully for the evening. He was wearing a shiny mauve plastic raincoat, a white party dress with a scoop neckline, white high-heeled shoes and white cotton gardening gloves. He'd applied generous amounts of pancake makeup and eye shadow, and his Chinese Red lipstick was a perfect match for the polish on his fingernails. Unfortunately the overall effect was spoiled for the moment by his shoulder-length platinum wig, which had been knocked askew as he'd climbed into the car.

Pursing his lips, the sniper angrily straightened the wig, taking pains to get it exactly right. When he was satisfied with his appearance he put the Honda in gear, brutally revved the engine, and then pulled out of the parking slot with a squeal of rubber. Accelerating fast, shifting into second, he drove hard towards the exit ramp, past the automatic sensor.

Clanking, the metal door of the garage rose like a stage curtain on a world washed grey with rain.

As the little car bounced over the curb and turned left on to Pendrell, the sniper leaned forward to switch on the windshield wipers and headlights. Through the rain-streaked side window he looked like one of those nearsighted old women with unsteady hands and a penchant for primary colours; the excessive amount of makeup and bright red lipstick suggestive of the face of a clown.

Due to the inclement weather and unusually sluggish Friday night traffic, the no. 3 bus arrived at the corner of Davie and Bute almost two minutes behind schedule. The front doors opened with an urgent hiss of compressed air, and Alice, furling her umbrella, stepped on board. Depositing her fare in the glass box next to the bearded driver, she asked for and received a transfer and then made her way slowly down the aisle.

11

There were less than a dozen passengers on the bus. Confronted with a wealth of choices, Alice hesitated and then sat down in the window seat opposite the rear exit. Hooking her umbrella over the chrome handrail in front of her, she unbuttoned her raincoat and took a well-thumbed paperback out of her purse. The oval face of the woman on the cover, framed by the hood of her dark green cloak, was delicate and pale. But her eyes were steady and her posture suggested an inner strength that Alice found appealing. She flipped through the book until she found her place, and began to read in the strong white glare of the overhead lights.

The yellow Honda bucked and lurched as it sped down the pothole-strewn lane that parallels the 1100 block West Broadway. As the car neared the end of the block it slowed sharply, and then swerved to pull up tight against the rear of an abandoned Shell station on the corner. The sniper switched off the lights and windscreen wipers, but left the motor running. With the black gun case cradled in his arms, he ran crouching through the rain towards the side door which provided access to the service bays. There was a fat brass padlock fastened to the door, but it was useless — the hasp had been violently torn from the wooden frame.

The sniper slipped into the empty building and stood with his head cocked to one side, listening. After a moment he walked cautiously but rapidly across the oil-slicked concrete floor towards the office at the front of the building.

Sheets of plywood put up to protect the plate glass windows had proved nothing more than a provocation to vandals. Broken glass crunched underfoot as the sniper made his way to a triangular gap between the overlapping sheets of wood. It was tough going in his high heels. He used the gun case as a balancing wand, and moved slowly.

From the window, the intersection of Broadway and Alder was no more than fifty metres away. Where the gas pumps had once stood there were now only a few rusty bolts thrusting up from the concrete island. The sniper's field of fire was clear and unobstructed. He saw that the traffic on Broadway was, as he had expected, not very heavy.

He turned away from the window towards the low counter that had once held the cash register. Having swept away a few shards of glass with his gloved hand, he gently put down the black leather case.

Out on the street the lights changed and the traffic suddenly pulled away, tires hissing anxiously on the wet asphalt.

The sniper unfastened two brass catches and opened the rifle case. The case was lined with red plush, and there were fitted spaces for the gun and telescopic sight, an extra pair of magazines. He dropped one of the magazines into a pocket of his raincoat, picked up the rifle and drew the bolt part way back. There was a cartridge in the chamber — brass gleamed in the dim light. There were two more rounds in the magazine; that gave him three shots before he would have to reload. Three would be more than enough. He slammed home the bolt, laid the rifle back down on the counter, and checked his watch.

It was twenty-eight minutes to nine. He was running a little late.

With a growing sense of urgency, he quickly pulled off his gloves and took a small clear plastic box out of an inner pocket of his raincoat. From it he removed one of a pair of earplugs made of soft pink wax. This he massaged between index finger and thumb until it was warm and soft, and then screwed it into his ear. Fumbling with the second piece of wax, he dropped the plastic box. He cursed softly, knelt to pick it up, stuffed it back into his pocket.

The wig got in his way as he tried to insert the second piece of wax. Furiously he brushed aside the coarse artificial hair, jammed the earplug in place. Now his watch showed that he had somehow fallen almost three minutes behind schedule. Rattled, he tried to force the gloves back on the wrong hands. He was sweating heavily. The wig made his scalp itch. He didn't know what he'd do if he missed her. He couldn't imagine waiting another week to try again.

Finally, without realizing quite how he had done it, he managed to get the gloves turned around and right side up. Under the white party dress he could feel his heart thumping rapidly. He was hyperventilating, his breathing was fast and shallow and he felt on the edge of panic, ready to fall apart. There was something else he had to do, but he couldn't think what it was. He wiped the sweat from his eyes, forced himself to calm down, to concentrate. After a long moment, he sighed deeply and then put on a pair of untinted Bausch & Lomb shooting glasses. Ready now, he picked up the Winchester and went back to the gap in the hoarding.

He was almost four full minutes behind schedule, but because of the traffic and the rain, so was the no. 3 bus.

The Redfield scope had been specifically designed for use under conditions of low light. Alice Palm's head, bisected by the cross hairs, was so crisp and clear that the sniper could see the detailing in the tiny gold cross dangling from her left ear. He flicked off the safety catch and pressed his cheek firmly against the walnut stock. At 2,150 feet per second, the muzzle velocity of the .460 Magnum is relatively slow for a modern weapon. But the bus was decelerating for the traffic light, and in any case the lead required at such short range was negligible.

The sniper sighted on the tip of Alice's nose, elevated the barrel a fraction of an inch, and gently squeezed the trigger. The rubber recoil pad slammed into his shoulder. The barrel jumped. Tendrils of dust drifted down from the ceiling. And despite the considerable protection offered by the earplugs, the thunderclap of the shot in that confined space was loud enough to make him wince with pain.

At the exact moment that the sniper fired, the traffic light turned from red to green. The bus driver, anticipating the change and anxious to get back on schedule, put his foot down on the gas pedal just in time to save Alice's life. The bullet punched a hole in the window no more than a quarter of an inch behind her head and on a level with her temple, instantly enveloping her in a fine cloud of safety glass. Glass sparkled on her shoulders, in her hair, across the pages of her book and on the empty seat beside her, on the floor. Startled and bewildered, she turned and peered out the window, into the soggy blackness of the night.

Half-blinded by the muzzle flash, the sniper worked the Winchester's bolt and pumped another round into the chamber.

14

Alice had just managed to work out what the hole in the window might mean when the second bullet smashed through the glass and struck her in the collarbone. The force of impact broke her neck, killing her instantly and tumbling her sideways off the seat and into the dirty wet aisle. She lay face down on the rubber mat, her body twisted awkwardly, the paperback still clutched tightly in her hand. Except for the bright red blood spouting energetically from a shredded aorta, she lay absolutely still.

The bus driver heard the thump of the body hitting the floor. He glanced in his rearview mirror, saw Alice and jumped on the brakes. The bus skidded to a halt in the middle of the intersection. The driver was halfway out of his seat when the vehicle lurched forward, throwing him against the windscreen. From the rear of the bus there was the sound of metal collapsing, and then the blare of a horn.

One of the passengers screamed.

In the murky gloom of the garage, the sniper tilted his rifle towards the ceiling, ejected the spent cartridge and caught it neatly in mid-air. Stooping, he hunted quickly through the rubble on the floor until he found the first cartridge. He stood both casings on end in the middle of the space he had cleared on the counter. Then he put the rifle and spare magazine back into the leather case and walked through the garage to the Honda idling quietly in the alley.

On the bus, the driver and passengers clustered silently around Alice's body. The driver crouched beside her, took her bloody wrist gingerly in his hand, and searched for a pulse. He continued to shift his thumb across her limp and slippery flesh until, belatedly, he realized that no one could possibly survive such a terrible wound, that the woman had to be dead. Perplexed and embarrassed, he glanced up at the ring of pale blank faces surrounding him. Then he gently removed the paperback from Alice's hand, marked the page, and shoved the book into her coat pocket.

II

THE POLICE CAFETERIA at 312 Main Street is bisected by a horseshoe-shaped self-service counter where prepared sandwiches, fresh fruit, and a limited choice of hot meals can be bought by hungry cops and support staff more concerned with their budgets than their taste buds. The usual offerings at the cafeteria include fried chicken, steak and kidney pie, and an almost supernaturally tasteless tuna casserole.

At ten minutes past nine on the night that Alice Palm was murdered, the cafeteria was empty except for a few uniformed patrolmen, a pair of junior clerks from the typing pool, and a homicide detective named David Ulysses Atkinson. Atkinson was making his way towards the cash register, carrying a plastic tray containing a large glass of milk and a limp slice of apple pie. His eye was on the girl behind the cash register, a skinny redhead named Lynda. She'd been working the night shift all week long, and Atkinson had spent a lot of time thinking about her, trying to work out the best way of hitting on her.

Atkinson was five foot eight inches tall, and very good at estimating heights. He guessed that Lynda was easily five-eleven, and maybe even a six-footer. Nothing turned him on like tall women. In heels, she'd be a knockout. As he approached the cash register he took a flat gold money clip out of his pants pocket, flipping his jacket well back to give her a peek at his weapon. Tonight he was packing his chrome-plated Colt .357 Magnum. The gun had an eight-inch barrel and fancy carved rosewood grips that he'd ordered by mail from a speciality shop in Los Angeles. The Colt was a very good-looking piece of machinery, flashy and lethal. In Atkinson's experience, the ladies rarely failed to be intrigued.

He waved the money clip over the tray and said, "What's the tab, honey?"

The pie was a dollar forty-five, the milk sixty cents. Ordinarily, the numbers wouldn't have given Lynda any trouble. But the way that Atkinson was looking at her made it a little hard to concentrate. Not that she particularly objected. She had to admit that the cop smiling up at her was kind of cute, even if he was a bit on the short side. He had a nice bone structure. Bedroom eyes. His curly black hair was thick and glossy, and beneath the pale blue fitted shirt his stomach looked hard and flat. Also, like many smallish men, he was an immaculate if somewhat conservative dresser. Clothes had always been a major item with Lynda; men who wore jeans didn't do a thing for her. She rang up the pie and milk on the cash register. Two dollars and five cents, as always.

Atkinson offered her a twenty-dollar bill. She made change and he added the bills to his clip without bothering to count them. Then he said, "What time you finish your shift?" just like that, no preliminaries, catching her by surprise.

"Why?" she said, off-balance.

"You like Italian food?"

"Maybe."

Atkinson gave her a big smile. His teeth were square and white. "You get off at eleven, am I right?"

Lynda nodded.

"Why don't I pick you up, we can go over to Il Giardino. Drink some wine, beat up a plate of veal." Atkinson sipped at his glass of milk. "You ever been there. To Il Giardino, I mean?"

Lynda shook her head, smiling demurely, and then glanced past Atkinson, over his shoulder.

Atkinson turned, wondering what had deflected her interest. He saw George Franklin lumbering towards him, weaving his way through the tables, bumping into chairs, apologizing to people without bothering to look at them. Atkinson's shoulders sagged. He muttered something Lynda pretended not to hear.

Franklin and Atkinson had been partners for a little over two years. Atkinson was still making adjustments. Although he liked tall women, he didn't care for big men at all. Franklin was six-two in his Argyle socks, never less than forty pounds overweight. As if this wasn't aggravation enough, Franklin was a lousy dresser. His suits were always a muddy brown colour, his shirts an uncertain white, his tie either too wide or too loud. To top it all off, there was always a cigarette dangling from the corner of Franklin's mouth, and he squinted perpetually, as if he couldn't quite believe what he was looking at.

"Dave," he said enthusiastically, still twenty feet away but closing fast. "Where the hell have you been the past half-hour? I've been looking all over for you!" When he spoke, the cigarette in his mouth jumped up and down in perfect sync with his words, as if it was the lever that was responsible for the opening and closing of his mouth. Ash tumbled from the cigarette, exploded on the rounded apex of his belly. He didn't seem to notice. He dropped a meaty, nicotine-stained hand on Atkinson's shoulder.

"Hey," said Atkinson. "Go mug somebody else." He pushed Franklin's hand away. "What's the matter, George, can't you see I'm in the middle of a conference?"

Franklin nodded hello to Lynda, being polite. To Atkinson he said, "There's a dead woman in a bus over on West Broadway."

"And she died of a broken heart, so naturally I'm your primary suspect."

"Actually," said Franklin, "she was shot with a large calibre rifle, and we got no suspects whatsoever."

Atkinson took a key ring out of his pocket. He separated one key from the rest, and dropped it on the counter.

"Key to your heart?" said Lynda.

"My apartment," said Atkinson. "Three-ten, twenty-one fifty Creelman. If I'm not back by the time you get off, you go on over there and make yourself comfy."

"I'll think about it, okay."

"Fine," said Atkinson. He smiled. "And when you've finished thinking about it, you get your cute little ass in gear." Before she could think of anything to say, Atkinson spun on his heel and started to make his way through the scattered tables towards the exit. Franklin picked up the abandoned glass of milk and drained it. No time, unfortunately, for the pie. A waste, but Atkinson probably hadn't intended to eat it anyway. He was too busy watching his weight to eat anything but celery sticks. No doubt the pie hadn't been anything but a ruse, something for Atkinson to hide behind while he snuck up on the redhead. Franklin

18

picked up a plastic fork and made a quick stab. Chewing, he hurried to catch up with his partner.

"Kind of skinny, isn't she?"

"Maybe she's got a way of making up for it," said Atkinson. "Tell me about the babe on the bus."

Franklin filled Atkinson in as the two detectives trotted up the stairs to the main floor, turned and headed down the wide hallway towards the Main Street exit of the building. As they approached the double glass doors, a homicide detective named Jack Willows pushed his way inside, his shoulders still hunched against the rain. He ignored Atkinson but nodded to Franklin.

"How's it going, George?"

"No complaints," said Franklin. "You seen Norm, lately?"

"He's holding his own."

"Say hello for me, will you. Tell him I'll be around as soon as I can make it."

"Tell him yourself, George," said Willows equably. Norm Burroughs was Willows' partner. For the past three months he'd been buried in the cancer ward of the Royal Columbian Hospital. During that time Willows had been the bearer of too many broken promises. If Franklin had anything to say to Burroughs, he could do it all by himself.

"Come on, George," said Atkinson. "We're on a case, let's get moving." He grinned mirthlessly at Willows. "There's a young lady waiting for us on a bus."

"I heard about her," said Willows. "She sounds like just your type."

The bus was still parked in the middle of the intersection. Within five minutes of the shooting it had been surrounded by squad cars, ghost cars, ambulances and fire department inhalators, even a big hook-and-ladder. All the noise and lights had quickly attracted a crowd. Now the civilian traffic was hopelessly snarled and the mass of pedestrians had swelled to the point of overflowing the sidewalk and spreading into the street. Franklin leaned on the horn as a zombie in a cream-coloured track-suit stumbled off the curb and into the path of their unmarked dark green Chevrolet.

19 —

"Teach him a lesson," said Atkinson. "Knock him flat."

"I'd love to, but I couldn't handle the paperwork."

In the glare of their headlights a cop wearing a black rainslicker marked with an abstract pattern of silver reflecting tape laid a string of flares along the flank of the bus. Off to the left, a corporal with the crossed pistols of a marksman on his sleeve struggled with a spool of yellow 'crime scene' plastic tape.

Atkinson pointed through the windscreen. "Over there, George."

Franklin nodded, turning the wheel.

The bus driver and passengers were standing in a tight cluster on the lee side of the bus, away from the traffic. The driver was compulsively explaining to a uniformed transit supervisor why he had stopped his vehicle in the intersection instead of following company regulations and pulling over to the curb. The supervisor listened with every appearance of sympathy, even though he was hearing the story for the third time nonstop, as if the driver's tongue had turned into a Mobius strip. The driver was in shock. The supervisor, arriving on the scene, had found him crouched over a puddle of rainwater, frantically rubbing Alice Palm's blood from the cuff of his shirt.

As Franklin braked the Chevrolet, the rear door of the bus opened, splashing light across the asphalt, and a pair of ambulance attendants carried the body of Alice Palm out on a folding stretcher.

"For Christ's sake," said Atkinson, "who told those two clowns they could move the body?"

"Beats me," said Franklin. He turned off the engine, reached across Atkinson to open the glove compartment, pulled out a thick wool toque. Atkinson glared at the toque with disgust, as if it had been made from the fur of an endangered species, pushed out of the car and slammed the door shut behind him. Franklin pulled the toque well down over his ears and turned up the collar of his coat. It was raining like a bitch. He got out of the car and trotted slowly and reluctantly after Atkinson, who was on a collision course with the stretcher.

The man at the rear of the stretcher heard Atkinson's heels on

20

the pavement. He took a quick look at Atkinson's face, stopped, and unzipped the bodybag without being told.

Atkinson peered down at Alice Palm's calm and lifeless face. Franklin came wheezing and puffing up behind him. Still looking down at the corpse, Atkinson said, "There's something funny going on here, George."

"What's that?" said Franklin.

"I don't know her." Atkinson smiled at the two ambulance attendants. They chuckled appreciatively. Atkinson punched the taller of the two lightly in the chest. "Who authorized you to move the body, asshole?"

"The bus guy, the one in the grey uniform, with the walkie."

"The supervisor?"

"Yeah, him."

"Something to look forward to," said Atkinson. "You'll probably be hearing from us."

Atkinson started towards the bus, Franklin tagging along behind. Atkinson waved at the passengers. "Look at them, standing there in the rain like a bunch of sheep."

"We can't put them back in the bus, they'd walk all over the evidence."

"What evidence is that, George?"

"Why don't we send them downtown. They can get some coffee, dry out a little, stay happy."

"Not a bad idea." Atkinson veered towards a motorcycle cop perched on his Harley. The cop was keeping himself busy listening to his radio. There had been a knifing in a Gastown bar. The dispatcher sounded as if his mouth was full of tinfoil. As Atkinson drew nearer, the cop turned to look at him. Water poured from the folds and creases in his raincape. He leaned forward to turn down the volume on the radio.

"I can see you got a lot on your hands," said Atkinson, "but there's something I want you to do for me. You see that bunch of people over there by the bus?"

"Yeah, I see them."

"Get their names, and then take them downtown. Wait for us until we get there. Think you can handle that?"

"What about my bike?"

Atkinson ignored him. "They're all material witnesses in a murder investigation, so don't lose anybody, understand?"

The cop nodded. Water dripped from the visor of his crash helmet, splashed into his lap. He watched the two detectives push through the slanting rain and then climb into the brightly illuminated bus. After a moment he dismounted stiffly from the Harley. A sudden gust of wind shook the overhead wires, and a handful of fat raindrops splattered across the broad saddle of the bike. The cop sighed, and trudged dispiritedly towards the passengers. Maybe he could borrow a squad car. Probably not.

Franklin followed Atkinson down the narrow aisle of the bus. The driver had left the heater on full blast. Despite the draft coming in through the shattered window, the vehicle was pleasantly warm. Franklin unbuttoned his raincoat, shook the water from his toque. He listened to the rain drumming on the metal roof, the muted squeaking of Atkinson's shoes on the rubber mat.

The outline of the body had been sketched on the floor in yellow chalk. Rainwater and blood had blurred the carefully drawn lines, but the effect, paradoxically, had been to somehow thrust the after-image of death into a sharper focus.

A little bit of yellow chalk. Hardly the shadow of a corpse. Certainly nothing Atkinson hadn't experienced a dozen times or more. And yet he was, for some reason he couldn't quite pin down, vaguely unnerved. He looked away, and saw Alice Palm's purse and umbrella lying on the seat among the fragments of glass from the window.

Atkinson picked up the purse, opened it, and sifted quickly through the contents. Loose change, the major credit cards, a driver's licence. Breath mints. Lipstick. Kleenex. And down at the bottom of this portable midden, two hundred dollars in crisp new twenties, and a three-pack of contraceptives. According to the licence, Alice Palm was forty-four years old. Atkinson, who considered himself something of an expert, deduced that she had been more concerned with disease than pregnancy. He snapped shut the purse. Aside from the roll of cash and the rubbers, there was nothing unusual about the contents. Not at first glance,

22

anyway. He and Franklin would take a much closer look when they got back to 312 Main, and then hand it all over to the crime lab.

Franklin, who had been crawling down the aisle on his hands and knees, came to the end of the bus and stood up.

"Find anything down there?" said Atkinson.

"Zilch." Franklin brushed ineffectually at his pants, wiped his hands on his raincoat.

Atkinson picked up the umbrella, swinging it by the handle. He did a thing with his feet, a little sideways shuffle. Detective Astaire. He tossed the purse to Franklin. "There's a couple of hundred bucks in there. Maybe you better lock it in the boot of the car before we find ourselves with another crime on our hands. He stepped carefully over the chalk lines and down into the stairwell. The rear doors hissed open. He looked up. "Is there a flashlight in the car, George?"

"Yeah, sure."

"Let's drop off the purse, grab the flash, and go take a look at the garage."

"Okay," said Franklin.

Atkinson stepped down from the bus, unfurled Alice Palm's umbrella with a theatrical flourish, and danced off into the rain. Franklin slung the purse over his shoulder. It was typical of his relationship with Atkinson that he had been the one left holding the bag.

There were seven of them squeezed into the squad car. The motorcycle cop, Earl Simpson, was behind the wheel. The transit supervisor was next to him and one of the passengers was pressed up against the far side window. The other three passengers and the bus driver were crammed into the back seat. The inside of the car was like a sauna, except hotter. There clearly wasn't room in the car for all seven of them. Simpson took it as a sign of his authority that, so far, no one had dared complain. He flipped open his notebook and carefully wrote down the time, date, and location. Then he twisted in his seat, pointed at the driver with the business end of his Bic, and said, "What's your name, pal?"

"Kenneth R. Stoddard," said the driver. He spoke as if he was already on the witness stand, the words slow and clear and a little too loud.

"What's your present address, Ken?"

Stoddard leaned forward, blinking rapidly. "Listen, there's something I have to tell you."

"What?" said Simpson.

"There was another passenger on the bus. Somebody who isn't here now."

Simpson chewed furiously on the end of his pen. "You mean he took off on me? Shit, why didn't somebody speak up?"

"No," said Stoddard, "he disappeared the minute I stopped the bus, right after the woman got shot."

Simpson relaxed. "That was before I got there, right?"

"Yeah, right."

"You just make sure you remember that," said Simpson. "Now, what did the guy look like?"

"He was built like a weight-lifter," said Stoddard. "He was wearing a black leather jacket and a Blue Jays baseball cap."

"Expos," said one of the other passengers, a woman in her seventies with short grey hair and bifocals thick as the bottom of a shot glass.

"You watch much baseball?" Simpson said to Stoddard.

"Once in a while, mostly around the playoffs."

"I never miss a game," said the woman. "I've even got a subscription to the Sports Network."

Simpson wrote 'Expos baseball cap' in his notebook in small block letters.

"Okay, so far we got a muscleman wearing a black leather jacket and a baseball cap. Anything else?"

"He had long blond hair," said the woman.

"Down to his shoulders," said Stoddard.

"Blue eyes," said a man in the back seat, a young Chinese guy with an earring.

"Green," said Stoddard.

"Blue," said the Chinese kid.

"Green," said the old woman.

"I'd swear they were blue," said another man, an old geezer

who could have been the woman's husband. "A real bright blue, like my granddaughter's."

Earl Simpson sat hunched in the seat with the tip of his pen hovering an inch above the paper. There was no way responsibility for the missing Expos fan could be blamed on him. But Earl knew that when the abbreviated cop with the cold eyes found out he was one passenger short of a load, he was going to have to kick somebody's ass. Inhuman nature. And in his heart of hearts, Earl Simpson knew exactly who that somebody was going to be.

There was a squad car parked in front of the oval concrete island where the gas pumps had once stood. As the two detectives passed through the twin beams of the headlights, Franklin waved his badge at the cop peering at them from behind the wheel.

"He knows who we are," said Atkinson.

"Courtesy, it's contagious."

"Sure thing, George."

They followed a narrow, crumbling sidewalk around to the rear of the garage. Franklin saw that squad cars had been stationed at each end of the alley, to keep it clear of civilian traffic. He made a mental note to find out who had positioned the cars, intending to give the man a word of thanks. He flashed the five-cell flashlight across the mud along the edges of the lane. He could see where a car had pulled over. The tyre tracks were already starting to crumble under the steady onslaught of the rain.

"We ought to get a tarp over that, or a piece of plywood, something."

Atkinson nodded his agreement. The rear door of the garage was wide open. He fingered the broken hasp. No rust where the screws had been torn free of the door frame. "We got a break and enter, as well as murder."

"Have to catch him first," said Franklin.

Atkinson furled his borrowed umbrella and they went into the building, following the beam of the flashlight and the lingering smell of cordite across a greasy black expanse of concrete and into the front office. Franklin held the light on the débris-strewn floor as Atkinson moved cautiously towards the gap in the hoarding, drawn like a moth towards the dim triangle of light, the rare opportunity to view the world from the perspective of a killer.

Standing where the shooter must have stood, Atkinson had a perfect view of the bus. The interior of the vehicle was so brightly lit that he could see the red splatter of blood on the paintwork on the far side of the aisle. As he stared out the window he slowly became aware of a soft thumping coming from somewhere behind him, a sound so steady and insistent it might have been the beating of his heart.

Turning, he saw the vague outline of a man sitting on the counter behind him. A surge of adrenalin made his heart leap. He dropped the umbrella and fumbled under his jacket for the chrome-plated Colt, at the same time crying out to Franklin, who brought the flashlight around in a wide, sweeping arc.

"It's about time you guys got here," said Jack Willows, squinting into the glare.

III

INSPECTOR HOMER BRADLEY'S crab-apple green office was on the third floor of 312 Main. The room was furnished with a large cherrywood desk, one leather chair and two plain wooden ones, and a pair of grey metal three-drawer filing cabinets. There was only one window in the office. It was small, faced north, and — until the beginning of the week — had offered a clear and unobstructed view of the brick wall of the adjoining building, less than six inches away.

When Bradley had first moved into the office, he'd found the almost total lack of natural light depressing, even a little claustrophobic. But during the five years he'd been in residence, he had gradually come to know every subtlety of coloration in the brick and every nuance of texture in the crumbling grey mortar. Without him ever knowing how or when it had happened, the wall had evolved into a complex work of art that never failed to change, however minutely, from one day to the next. On more than one occasion an unexpected visitor had entered the office to find Bradley standing at the little window, studying the wall as if it were a valuable and much-admired painting.

And now the wall was gone. Reduced in less than a week to an untidy heap of rubble, a dusty memory.

Bradley drained his coffee cup and put it down on the windowsill. With his hands in his pockets, he stared out over the brooding expanse of the harbour. The water was matt black, pounded flat by the rain. In the background, the greyish-blue bulk of the North Shore mountains seemed to crouch under the sagging, bloated belly of the clouds.

The view was quiet as a photograph, wonderfully gloomy and morose, perfectly suited to Bradley's mood. Reluctantly, he went over to his desk and sat down. A dozen colour photographs lay spread out on his blotter. Alice Palm gazed incuriously up at him through a dozen sets of glazed and foggy eyes. He shuffled the photographs into a neat pile and put them to one side. Glancing up, he caught Jack Willows watching him. The expression in Willows' eyes wasn't all that different from Alice Palm's. He looked bored, as if he was waiting for a bus. He was leaning against the crab-apple wall, his hands folded across his chest. During the five long minutes Bradley had kept him waiting, he hadn't said a word or moved an inch. The boy was on his best behaviour, and Bradley knew why. He leaned forward in his chair and flipped open the lid of the Haida-carved cedar humidor his wife had given him on 24th January 1982, the day their divorce had been finalized. He chose a cigar, fished a big wooden kitchen match out of the breast pocket of his suit jacket, and lit up. When he had the cigar burning evenly, he waved the match into extinction and flipped it into the metal wastebasket next to his desk. Willows, a reformed smoker, stared impassively into the middle distance. No need to offer the box around.

There was a light knock on the door. It swung open and a young woman walked confidently into the office. He had never seen her before, but Bradley recognized her immediately: her file had been languishing in his in-tray for the better part of a month.

"Parker?"

Claire Parker nodded, and shut the door.

Bradley motioned towards the wooden chairs. "Sit down, make yourself comfortable."

Parker glanced at Willows, back to Bradley. "No thanks, I'd rather stand."

Bradley shrugged, a little irritated but not letting it show. According to the file, Parker was twenty-eight years old, five foot seven inches tall, weighed one hundred and seven pounds, and had a pale complexion, dark brown eyes and black hair.

Well, the file hadn't given him the whole story by a long shot. There was no hint, for example, that Parker's eyes were unusually large, dark as chocolate, liquid and expressive, full of warmth and intelligence. Or that her hair fell in a glossy mass, framing a delicate oval face, generous mouth, a nose that was strong and firm and full of character. If Parker's file had mentioned the Taj Mahal all it probably would have said was that it was a building in India.

Bradley found himself wondering what kind of body Parker had tucked away under her loosely-cut grey tweed jacket and matching skirt. He'd noticed that she had terrific ankles. In his reasonably varied experience that was usually a promising sign.

Not that he imagined she'd be all that interested in a short balding pear-shaped fifty-two-year-old twice-divorced lapsed Catholic. Although, of course, you never could tell.

Bradley waved his cigar at Willows, a sort of informal benediction. "Jack, this is Claire Parker. Claire, Jack Willows."

"Hi," said Parker.

Willows nodded politely, and then turned to look out the window at the matt-black water, and the clouds.

Bradley leaned back in his chair, taking solace in the familiar creaking of the leather. When Norm Burroughs made the abrupt switch from the homicide squad to the cancer ward, Bradley had allowed a decent interval to pass and then started sniffing around for a replacement. A desk sergeant at the Oakridge Substation had tipped him to Parker. Heavy on formal education, she had put in very little time on the street. Bradley had thought about it for a few days and then arranged the transfer. Parker's lack of seasoning worried him a little, but he knew that anyone paired off with Jack Willows would soon have enough experience to last a lifetime — if she managed to live that long.

"Jack," said Bradley, "Claire is your new partner."

"I don't need a new partner," said Willows. "The old one isn't dead yet."

Bradley flicked an inch of cigar ash into the wastebasket. "Maybe not, but you and I both know he might as well be."

"What's this all about?" said Parker.

Bradley ignored her.

The door opened and George Franklin shuffled into the office. He yawned, covered his mouth with his hand, waved a genial hello.

Bradley's fingers drummed on the stack of photographs. "You're due some time off, Jack. If you want to take it now, it's okay by me."

29

Willows went over to the window and stared venomously out at the harbour. Cloud had completely obscured the mountains. Tendrils of mist trailed down into the ocean. The rain was coming down so heavily that it was impossible to tell where the sea left off and the land began. He pressed his forehead against the cold pane of glass, felt it vibrate under a sudden gust of wind. He wanted a slice of the Alice Palm cake so badly that he was even willing to take Parker along for the ride. There was no point in telling himself otherwise. He hoped Norm Burroughs would understand.

Bradley introduced Parker to Franklin. He asked Franklin where Dave Atkinson was.

"On his way," said Franklin vaguely. "Should be here any minute."

"That's real considerate of him," said Bradley. He glared angrily at Franklin until Franklin looked away, and then he began to sort through the photographs of Alice Palm, searching for a detail he might have missed, some small thing.

It was five minutes before Atkinson made it to the office. The first thing he said was, "What the hell is he doing here?"

"Waiting," said Willows.

"Shut the door," said Bradley.

Atkinson gave the door a push. The square of frosted glass rattled.

Bradley waved his cigar at Parker. "Have you two met, Dave?"

"In the elevator," said Atkinson. "About an hour ago."

"Really?" said Parker, clearly not remembering.

"Look," Atkinson said to Bradley, "George and I answered the squeal. We examined the body, collected and tagged the evidence. It was me and George who conducted the initial investigation, standing around in the rain, sneezing. We worked hard on this one, Inspector. Christ, we were stuck in the squadroom questioning dumb-ass witnesses and drinking shitty coffee until two o'clock in the morning."

"What's the point, Dave?"

"The point is, what's Willows doing here? The Alice Palm case belongs to us."

"Is that right, Dave?"

Atkinson hesitated, decided to keep his mouth shut.

"I'm in charge of the manpower," said Bradley. "What square you stand on. How long you stay there. Where you jump next." He looked around the room, softening the blow to Atkinson's pride by speaking to everyone. "That's the way it is, that's the way it's always going to be."

Willows turned away from the window, wondering what was coming next.

"What've you got so far?" Bradley asked Atkinson.

"Not much. The body. Shell casings, bullet fragments. All we're sure of is that a person or persons unknown shot Alice Palm for a reason or reasons unknown."

"What you're saying is that it was personal, there's no chance she was the victim of a random shooting."

"Yeah, right."

"How did you happen to come to that conclusion, Dave?"

Atkinson was very much aware that Willows was giving him all of his attention, listening to everything he said. He chose his words carefully, occasionally glancing at Franklin for support.

"For starters, neither George nor I have ever heard of a pro using such a large calibre weapon. A gun like the .460 Magnum has way too many disadvantages."

"For example?"

"Ammunition is hard to come by. Depending on the manufacturer, the magazine holds only two or at the most three rounds. The weapon makes a hell of a racket. It's next to impossible to conceal. What else? Velocity is real slow, and the bullet has a trajectory like spit."

"Another thing," said Franklin. "The two spent cartridges we found in the garage were very shiny, a lot shinier than you'd expect. We sent them to the lab. Jerry Goldstein found traces of Brasso around the flange and in the area of the primer, in that little groove between the two pieces of metal."

Bradley took the cigar out of his mouth. "You're telling me the shooter sat down with a rag and a can of Brasso and put a nice shine on his bullets before he went out and blew a hole the size of a doughnut in Alice Palm?"

31

"That's what it looks like."

"Weird," said Bradley. "What else have you got, if anything?"

Franklin took a much-travelled notebook out of the inside pocket of his suit jacket. He licked the ball of his thumb and flipped through the pages until he came to his notes on Alice Palm. The pages were wrinkled where the rain had dampened them, but his writing was round and modest, unhurried. He squinted at the page for a moment, and then fumbled through his pockets until he found his glasses.

Atkinson sighed audibly.

Bradley dropped another inch of cigar ash into his wastebasket. He fiddled with the humidor until it was lined up just so.

Parker risked a quick glance at Willows, perched now on the windowsill, settled in.

Franklin shook his glasses out of a black imitation leather case, tilted his head slightly to one side as he put them on. The frames were rectangular, heavy, made of black plastic.

Parker thought the glasses had a nice effect. They somehow made Franklin look more dignified, even scholarly. He happened to glance up, and their eyes met. He gave her a brief, meaningless smile, and began to read.

"Alice Palm was a spinster. She was forty-four years old and as far as we know has no surviving relatives. She lived alone at The Berkely, 990 Bute. For the past twenty years she's been employed as a secretary at Foster Pharmaceuticals, over on West Pender. Her boss's name is Malcolm Armstrong. He's been with Foster a little over five years. Claims the victim was one of those quiet, dependable types that everybody liked, but nobody liked enough to get to know on an after-hours basis. Claimed he couldn't think of anybody who might have wanted her dead."

"No boyfriends?" said Bradley.

"Not that anybody at the office ever knew of," said Franklin. "But the answer to your question is a big fat yes." He peered over the tops of his glasses as he turned to the next page, and was gratified to see that he had everyone's attention. Franklin was famous for his notes, which by department standards were remarkably lucid and concise.

"Dave and I talked to the manager of The Berkely. Her

32

name's Collette Ringwood. She's a widow, in her mid-sixties, and has lived right across the hall from Alice Palm since the summer of 1962." Franklin smiled. "If you ever happen to be in the neighbourhood, drop in and try one of her home-made chocolate chip cookies. Take it from me, they're real tasty."

"I can believe it," said Bradley, gazing pointedly at Franklin's rotund belly.

Franklin buttoned up his jacket, and pressed on. "We kind of hoped that Collette, being the manager and all, might've kept her nose to the keyhole, so to speak. But it turns out the old girl is a TV junkie. Spends all day sitting in front of her Marconi, the sound turned up as loud as it'll go."

"What is she, deaf?" said Bradley.

"Got a hearing aid but she doesn't wear it much, due to the outlandish price of batteries."

"So, except for the free cookies, you got nothing."

"No, Inspector, we got lucky. There's another tenant in the building, a pensioner named Arnold Hooper, who does spend all his time prowling up and down the halls. Hooper told us that, for a quote modern young woman unquote, Alice Palm led a very quiet life. But every Friday night, no exceptions, she got all dressed up and went outside to play."

"Where?" said Parker.

Franklin turned to her in surprise, as if he had forgotten she was there. The heavy black glasses slipped down the bridge of his nose. "Hooper said he must've asked her that same question a hundred times or more, and never once got a straight answer. But wherever she went, there must have been men around."

"Why is that?" said Bradley.

"Because every once in a while she brought one home."

"A different guy every time," said Atkinson. "Never the same one twice."

"Or so Hooper says," added Franklin.

"If she was picking up strange guys all the time," said Atkinson, "that would account for the pack of rubbers we found in her purse." He glanced over at Parker, as if he expected a request for an explanation.

Franklin pushed his glasses back up on his nose, lit a cigarette

33

and turned the page. "Okay, as mentioned previously, the victim was shot with a rifle, calibre .460 Magnum. There were plenty of copper and lead alloy fragments in the body, but unfortunately we were unable to come up with the bullet."

"Why not?" Bradley again, a little impatient.

"Two shots were fired. The first went in one side of the bus and out the other. The second, ditto, except it also went through the victim. Judging from the angle of fire, both rounds went straight up Alder Street, maybe for a mile or more. But we took the spent cartridges down to the armory and showed them to Bernie Sparrows. Bernie wasn't positive, but he doubted if it was standard factory issue ammunition."

"You mean it was hand-loaded?"

"Bernie took the cartridges over to forensics first thing this morning. Goldstein told him he'd be able to tell if they were hand-loaded by analysing the powder residue and the crimp marks. But it's going to take him a day or two."

"As always."

"Anyway," said Franklin, "whatever results Goldstein comes up with, I think we can assume that we're butting heads with somebody who really knows his oats. The weird gun, the way the whole thing was set up. . . ."

"The ground where the car was parked," said Atkinson, "was just as wet as everywhere else in the alley. That means the car couldn't have been there more than a few minutes. The shooter knew Alice Palm's schedule right down to the last second. He knew exactly where to be and when to be there. He had her wired."

"What about the other passengers on the bus, you get anything out of them?"

"Names and addresses, not much more. One of them saw the muzzle flash, thought somebody was in there with a butane lighter, some kid fooling around. Otherwise, zilch."

Bradley lifted an eyebrow. "Nothing?"

"So far," said Franklin apologetically. He shut his notebook, removed his glasses, and vigorously massaged his nose.

"Wait a minute," said Willows. "What about the guy who took a hike?"

"What guy?" said Bradley.

"The skinny blond guy wearing a black leather jacket, baseball cap, and orange running shoes."

Franklin and Atkinson exchanged a quick look. They had talked it over at length and Atkinson had finally convinced Franklin to forget about the missing witness, reasoning that it was a loose end they would never track down and that what Bradley didn't know couldn't hurt them. Now Atkinson glared angrily at Willows, wondering where he had picked up his information. "As a matter of fact," Atkinson said to Bradley, "George and I aren't all that sure there was somebody else on the bus. At least, not at the actual time of the shooting. There was a lot of confusion — no one was willing to say exactly when he got off."

"But he might have been on board when the shots were fired, right?"

"It's a possibility," admitted Franklin after a pause. "That's why we've arranged for the driver and passengers to come down and take a walk through the mug books."

"When?"

"Well, we haven't worked out specific times just yet," said Franklin lamely.

"I'll just bet," said Bradley.

Atkinson tried to pick up the slack. "If they can't find him in the mug books, we'll get together with Steve Bozak and see if we can come up with a decent composite drawing. But to tell you the truth, Inspector, neither George nor I expect much to come of it."

"Why not?"

"Because the five people who claim they saw him can't agree on anything they say about him, except for his hair colour and the fact that he was wearing a baseball cap. They can't even agree on the colour of his eyes, for Christ's sake. Three of them swear they were green, the other two are positive they were blue."

"Maybe he's got one of each colour," said Bradley. "Like Fritz, my ex sister-in-law's cat." He noticed that his cigar had gone out, re-lit it with another kitchen match, flicked a speck of tobacco off his thumbnail. He knew damn well that if Willows

35

hadn't mentioned the lost witness, he'd never have found out about him. He also knew that Franklin and Atkinson had no intention of hauling out the mug books or calling on Bozak. They were both experienced cops; they'd decided that the missing blond was a dead end and not worth pursuing. Bradley couldn't fault their judgement but he didn't like the fact that they'd tried to slip one past him. Well, it was all bullshit. When he'd accepted his promotion and the desk that had gone with it, he'd traded in his gun for a shovel. "What about the car?" he said through a cloud of cigar smoke.

"We took casts of the tyre tracks in the mud behind the garage," said Atkinson. "And we measured the wheel span as indicated by the ruts. Goldstein is pretty sure the tyres were twelve-inch radials and that the car was probably a Honda Civic. Based on the tread wear, Goldstein estimates the car has forty or maybe fifty thousand miles on it."

"Which would make it what, three or four years old?"

"Somewhere in there."

"Any idea how many three or four year-old Honda Civics there are registered in the city?"

"Not yet. We're working on it."

"In the hundreds?"

"Or more." Atkinson smiled at Parker. "The car is real popular with the ladies, because it's so small, and easy to park."

"I suppose," Parker shot back, "that those same character-istics could account for your own success with the fairer sex."

Willows laughed out loud, and Atkinson gave him a look of pure malice.

Wearily, Bradley massaged his temples. "Okay," he said. "Dave, you and George are convinced that Alice Palm is dead because somebody wanted her dead, am I right?"

"Yeah, right."

"I tend to agree with you," said Bradley. "But Jack has another theory. Kind of an interesting one. He thinks the victim died as a result of a random shooting, and that the killer is going to hit again, that we've got a serial murderer on our hands."

"Wait a minute," said Atkinson. "There were half a dozen

people on that bus. If it was a random shooting, why did the killer fire twice at the same person?"

"Because he missed the first time," said Willows. He had been looking out of the window but now he turned to Atkinson and said, "I'd have thought that was fairly obvious, Dave."

"It's crap, that's what it is. You and your cute new partner are reaching, trying to grab a piece of my case."

"I thought we were all part of the same team," said Willows, smiling.

"No question about it," said Bradley. "Dave, you and George concentrate on the ammunition. Where did it come from? Who sold it and who bought it?" Bradley turned to Willows. "Jack, the first thing I want you to do is track down the missing baseball fan."

"Fine by me," said Willows.

Much to Bradley's surprise.

"What about the Honda?" said Parker.

"We'll take care of it," said Atkinson quickly.

Bradley mashed the remains of his cigar in his ashtray and emptied the ashtray into his wastebasket. "Anybody have any questions?"

Willows started for the door. Atkinson shook his head, no. He and Franklin had been given the hottest lead in the case. Willows and Parker, on the other hand, had been sent after a witness they might never bring to earth and who was almost certainly of no importance anyway. Atkinson would have preferred it if Willows had been kicked right out of the office, but the way it'd worked out wasn't too bad. When Atkinson nailed the shooter, it would be nice to rub it in Willows' face.

Bradley swivelled his chair around to face the window, putting his back to all of them, the whole feisty and snarling crew. He wondered what his new wall would be like. Concrete, no doubt. A flat and featureless slab of grey. Nervously twisting the ruby ring on the little finger of his left hand, he leaned back in his chair.

He hadn't thought it politic to mention it at the time, but Bradley agreed completely with Willows' pessimistic view of the case. The malevolent decision to use the powerful and brutally destructive .460 Magnum had not been made by the kind of man who would be satisfied with a single death. Bradley knew, his policeman's instinct promised him, that although Alice Palm had been the first victim, she wasn't going to be the last.

IV

THE GENTLY CURVING street was flanked on both sides by mature plane trees, the interlaced branches heavy with accumulated rain and thick with pale green buds. Willows was slouched silently in the passenger seat of the cream Ford, his brogues up on the dashboard. Parker was behind the wheel.

They were driving through the heart of Shaughnessy, one of the city's oldest and most prestigious neighbourhoods. The massive Victorian houses on their quarter-acre lots had once belonged only to the very rich, but now most of them had been subdivided into half a dozen or more small apartments, scaled to the comparatively modest requirements of the very middle class.

"Fantastic architecture," said Parker as they drove past a particularly large and imposing structure.

Willows grunted monosyllabically.

"I always liked looking at buildings. Maybe I should have been an architect."

"Could be," said Willows, obviously disinterested.

The overhanging branches of the plane trees screened out so much of the rain that the windshield wipers weren't able to work properly. The rubber blades shuddered in the middle of each arc, smearing the scattered drops of rain across the glass as if they were exotic little insects — soft and fragile creatures of liquid crystal. Parker concentrated on her driving for a few minutes and then said, "The missing baseball player, Shelley Rice. How did you get his name?"

"He phoned 312 Main and gave it to the duty officer. The duty officer gave it to me."

"Why you, instead of Franklin or Atkinson. Didn't he know it was their case?"

"He knew, all right. But he owed me a favour, and now he doesn't."

39

Willows' feet were still up on the dashboard. Parker noticed that although both his socks were dark blue, they didn't quite match. "Another thing," she said. "When Bradley was handing out the assignments, why didn't you tell him you already had Rice's name and address?"

"Because then he would've come up with some other way of wasting our time."

"What do you mean?" said Parker.

"Rice doesn't know anything about the murder. How could he? The only reason we're going to bother talking to him is so we can say we've done it."

"I don't understand. Why would Bradley deliberately give you something useless to do, why would he want to waste your time?"

"He thinks I'm emotionally distraught. He wants to keep me busy because it's his idea of therapy. But at the same time, he doesn't want to give me anything important to do because he doesn't want me screwing up the case."

"How could you do that?"

"Believe me, there are a million ways."

"What are we going to do after we finish with Rice?"

"We'll think of something," said Willows. "Turn left at the next corner."

"Whatever you say."

Parker braced herself, spun the wheel hard and slammed the gas pedal to the floor. The back tyres whined and slithered on the wet asphalt, and the rear end of the Ford broke free, drifting sideways. Willows clutched wildly at the dashboard. The heel of his shoe left a black streak across the windscreen. Parker steered expertly into the skid. When they were around the corner and the Ford had straightened she reached across the seat and jabbed Willows in the arm.

"Look, I heard about your partner, and I'm sorry. I'm sorry he's got cancer and I'm sorry it's killing him. I know this must be very hard on you."

"I don't want to talk about Norm," said Willows.

"That's right, and I don't like your attitude. Listen, I think it'd be great if a miracle happened, so the two of you could go live happily ever after in some cute little gingerbread house in the woods."

"What?" said Willows.

"But if it doesn't work out that way, and you end up getting stuck with me, try to remember something, will you? It isn't my fault."

"You finished?" said Willows.

"That depends."

"On what?"

"On you," said Parker.

Shelley Rice's house was brick, three storeys high, with a lot of leaded glass windows and a brand new cedar shake roof. The house stood squarely in the middle of a hundred-foot lot, and was surrounded by a low ornamental wall, also of brick. Parker pulled the Ford neatly up to the curb. Willows was out of the car before she'd killed the engine, slamming his door and moving purposefully towards the house. Parker locked her door, dropped the keys in her purse and followed Willows across the lush, manicured grass of the boulevard towards a black wrought-iron gate.

Willows fiddled with the latch, which was stiff with a fresh coat of paint. Parker caught up with him as he pushed the gate open. They walked side by side towards the house, along a path that wandered pointlessly across the lawn. As they climbed the steps towards the wide front porch, Willows discreetly loosened the snubnose Smith & Wesson in the clamshell holster clipped to his belt.

There was a brass knocker screwed to the door, an art nouveau likeness of a young girl's face. There was an air about her of dissipation and neglect. The once-clean and graceful lines of her face had been blurred and pitted by the passage of time. Her cheeks were badly corroded, her lips faded and slack. A greenish residue clogged her long and artfully tangled hair, stained the corners of her eyes. Willows hesitated, and then rapped his fist on the white-painted wood of the door.

Water dripped in a steady stream from a broken drainpipe to the porch railing, splattered across a rusting ten-speed bicycle.

41

Shelley Rice opened the door.

Willows estimated Rice's age at about twenty-five, his height at six foot even and his weight at roughly a hundred and seventy pounds. Rice had medium-length hair, a friendly, open face. He was wearing a black T-shirt, grey corduroy pants. Looking for the orange running shoes, Willows saw that his feet were bare. But like Fritz the cat, Rice had one eye of blue and one of green.

Rice ignored Willows. Smiling easily at Parker, he said, "It's the cops, am I right?"

"So far," said Willows.

Rice gave Parker another chance to admire his teeth. "Come on in, don't just stand there looking gorgeous."

Willows took a quick step towards Rice. As Rice automatically began to back away, Willows put the palm of his hand against Rice's chest and gave him a gentle push. Caught off-balance, Rice staggered back into the house. Inexplicably, he was still smiling.

Willows brushed past Rice and walked down a short hallway, turned left through a pair of French windows into the living room. There were Persian carpets on the oak floor. An over-stuffed Chesterfield and two matching chairs were clustered around a massive fieldstone fireplace. A pink marble lamp stood on an antique Chinese endtable.

Willows went through a curved archway into the dining room. There was twelve feet of mahogany table, eight matching chairs. A pine sideboard from eighteenth-century Quebec and a tea trolley just like the one his grandmother used to have. He moved down the length of the gleaming table to the huge floor-to-ceiling leaded glass windows that flooded the room with light. Standing at the windows, he could see all the way across the city and the harbour to the scattering of pastel highrises along the West Vancouver waterfront.

He didn't have to take a deep breath to smell it, the house reeked of money. He wondered who owned it. Not Shelley Rice, with his black T-shirt and bright orange shoes. Rice would toss the Persian carpets in the garbage and buy a couple of hundred yards of purple shag.

Willows heard the front door slam shut, and went back into the living room. Rice and Parker came through the French window. Rice still hadn't abandoned his smile. He looked directly at Willows and said, "Would anyone care for a drink?"

"Up against the wall," said Willows. "Hands in the air and legs spread wide."

Rice's smile faded. He stood there, looking dumb.

Willows pulled his revolver and pointed it at Rice's chest. "Move it, kid."

Rice swallowed noisily. He started to say something and then thought better of it and went over to the nearest wall and leaned into it. His left hand smeared the glass on a framed Toni Only watercolour. He glanced up, made a small sound of dismay, and shuffled sideways.

"Frisk him," Willows said to Parker.

Parker moved in on Rice.

"Jesus," said Rice weakly. "Is this legal?"

"I doubt it," said Willows. "Probably that's why we're all having so much fun."

Parker searched Rice quickly and efficiently, and then stepped away from him, out of the line of fire. With the look on Willows' face, she believed he was ready to shoot. "He's clean," she said.

"Sure he is. He's so fucking clean, he squeaks."

"Can I turn around now?" said Rice.

"If you're sure you want to."

Rice slowly lowered his arms. He turned around, his eyes avoiding Parker. He stared at the weapon dangling loosely from Willows' hand, the short barrel pointing at the oak floor. "You don't need that," he said. "I called you, remember?"

Willows studied Rice indifferently for a moment, and then put away the gun. "The question is, why did you do it?"

"Because I'm a good citizen." Nobody laughed. Rice shrugged. "You must've dusted down every last square inch of that bus, right?"

"Got a prior, Shelley?"

"You guessed it."

"What?"

"The worst. Took a shot at a guy."

43

"Hit him?"

"In the kneecap."

"What kind of gun you use?"

"A .22, a Hi-Standard automatic."

"When was that, Shelley?"

"Two years ago. I did fourteen months, I'm still on parole."
He paused, and then added, "I wasn't even trying to hit the guy,
just scare him a little."

"Why?"

Rice hesitated. "We had a business disagreement, I guess you
could say."

"Drugs?"

"Soft drugs. Nothing heavy."

"Anything else?"

"What d'you mean?"

"Convictions."

"No, nothing."

"You sure?"

"Absolutely. You don't believe me, go ahead and check."

"Who owns the house?"

"My dad. He's in Hawaii, on vacation."

"So that's why you turned yourself in, because we had your
prints and you knew we'd get to you sooner or later, so why not
do it now, because this way your old man never finds out about
it."

"You're way ahead of me," said Rice.

Parker stood quietly to the side, watching Willows ply his
trade. She wondered what he was getting at. Rice seemed to
know — the armpits of his T-shirt were dark with sweat.

"How old are you, kid?"

"Twenty-six."

"You working?"

"No, I'm unemployed. But who isn't, right?"

"What were you doing on the bus?"

"My car broke down. I was on my way home."

"The Jaguar in the carport around by the side of the house, is
that yours?"

Rice nodded.

"Expensive car. What went wrong?"

"It was nothing, a dead battery. I left my lights on."

"Okay," said Willows, "let's see if I follow you so far. You wanted to get home but your car wouldn't start because the battery was dead. So you grabbed a bus."

Rice frowned, nodded hesitantly. He looked, thought Parker, like a man trying to follow a vitally important conversation conducted in a foreign language.

"Kind of taking the long way around, weren't you? Heading east instead of south."

"I'm not all that familiar with the public transit system, to tell you the truth."

"When did you get the battery charged?"

"First thing this morning."

"What did you do, call a tow truck?"

"No, a friend of mine drove me back downtown. We used his jumper cables."

"What's the friend's name?"

Rice glanced at Parker, almost as if he hoped she might prompt him, now that the questions were getting tough.

"Come on now," said Willows. "You really expect me to shovel such low-grade shit? Your thirty-thousand-dollar car breaks down and instead of spending ten bucks on a taxi, you stand around in the rain waiting for a bus that's headed in the wrong direction?"

Willows moved rapidly towards Rice. His arm shot out. Rice flinched. Willows straightened the Toni Only hanging crookedly on the wall, giving the painting all his attention. Rice sagged with relief.

"I'm with homicide," said Willows. "Not narcotics. But if you don't tell me what you were doing on that bus, I'm going to phone downtown for the wrecking crew and the dogs. Your daddy's going to get back from the beach and find his house in pieces."

Rice paled. "Even if I was dealing, you think I'd be stupid enough to stash anything here?"

"Stupid enough or smart enough."

Rice studied the carpet beneath his feet, almost as if he

thought he might find the solution to his problems woven into the pattern of muted colours.

"Okay," he said at last, "I was on the bus to do some business."

"Who with?"

"I give you a name, it's the same as if I punched myself in the mouth until all my teeth fell out. You understand what I'm saying? I'd get hurt."

"If you don't give us a name, how are we going to confirm what you say?"

Rice spread his arms wide, a gesture of helplessness. "What if I saw something last night, something that could help you with the shooter?"

"Depends what it was."

"Hey, aren't we both supposed to bend a little?" Giving Willows a wide berth, Rice went over to the chair closest to the fireplace, and sat down. "As soon as the bus stopped, I jumped out. I wasn't sure if that woman was dead or what, but I'd heard the shot and I knew I had to get out of there. I mean, I was carrying enough of a load to get me sent so far up shit creek it'd never even been surveyed." Rice drummed his fingers nervously on the arm of the chair. "Anyhow, right after the bus stopped, it got hit by a car. Rear-ended. That jammed up the traffic and gave me a chance to scoot across to the other side of the street."

"Towards the gas station," said Parker.

"Yeah, right."

"What did you see, Shelley?" said Willows.

"A yellow Honda. One of the real small ones, a Civic."

"You get the plate number?"

"No. I couldn't even tell you if it had plates."

"You notice anything unusual about the car? A dent or scrape, rust, maybe a decal on the window, anything at all?"

"Nothing." Rice paused, and then, trying hard to play it casual, flashed his whole card. "I was too busy looking at the driver to pay any attention to the car."

"You saw the driver, is that what you're telling me? That you saw the driver?"

"That's right."

"What did he look like?"

46

"It wasn't a man. It was a woman."

Willows stared at him. "A woman?"

"It was dark, and it was raining, and the car was moving along at a pretty good clip. But the driver was a blonde, wearing a lot of makeup, and she was old."

"How old?"

"Old enough to be my grandmother," said Rice. He leaned back against the chair and closed his eyes, exhausted.

V

AT THE TENDER age of eighteen, Phasia Palinkas had kissed her parents goodbye and emigrated from sunny Thyrea to rainy Vancouver, travelling all those thousands of lonely miles from the shores of the Aegean to marry her childhood sweetheart, Giorgio.

Nine years later the childhood sweetheart misjudged a curve in the highway on his way home from an evening spent at a suburban bar. His late model Subaru slewed broadside across a grass divider and three lanes of oncoming traffic, hit a drainage ditch and rolled. Giorgio's door popped open and was torn free as the Subaru cartwheeled spectacularly into a thick stand of young alder. The trees shattered with the sound of a ragged volley of pistol shots. The Subaru came to rest on its side. Fastened in place by his seatbelt, Giorgio was pierced through and through by the sharp, jagged stumps.

The widow Palinkas soon discovered that because of her late husband's constant efforts to expand, his construction business was cash poor. Giorgio had borrowed heavily against his life insurance. The house had been remortgaged and the monthly payments were immense. There was a little money in the bank, but not much. Five minutes with the accountants convinced her that by the time the creditors had finally finished picking over the crumbs, her plate would be spotlessly clean.

Within six months she had sold the house and moved her two young daughters from the pleasant tree-lined streets of Kitsilano to a modest two-bedroom apartment in a stucco block on East Eleventh. The building was old, but clean. The rent was much cheaper than it would have been on the West Side. There was even a Greek community of sorts, though it was smaller and poorer than the one in her old neighbourhood.

But the main reason she'd moved to the apartment on East

Eleventh was because it was just around the corner from her new business — a decaying pool hall on Commercial Drive.

She still hardly knew how she'd come to own the pool hall. But if the decision to buy had been made partly as a consequence of her belief in the work ethic and the immutable value of land, it was also due to her luck in happening across a particularly handsome and persuasive real estate agent.

Her first month as a businesswoman was spent overseeing the many renovations she felt were necessary. The drab interior of the pool hall was transformed by a fresh coat of cream paint, more lights, a carpet salvaged from a demolished office building. Three pool tables were replaced by five of the smaller — and more lucrative — fooseball tables. Video games were installed next to the door, in full view of the street. And, finally, Phasia Palinkas lengthened the coffee shop counter and added half a dozen more stools. It was this last move that was most responsible for her sudden success. Her home cooking was excellent, her prices low. If her customers sometimes dawdled too long over their capuccino, she never seemed to notice.

Within a month of opening, her gross had tripled and she was showing a substantial profit.

On Saturdays, she closed at midnight. By quarter to twelve that night, there were only two customers left in the pool hall. Apostolos and Nichos were both regulars. Both men were in their late thirties, a bit overweight, prematurely balding. They looked so much alike that they were often mistaken for brothers.

Phasia Palinkas glanced up at the clock over the sink. Nichos was fiddling with a fooseball machine, twirling one of the protruding metal handles and making a brightly coloured row of plastic players twitch and wiggle like a chorus line. Apostolos was sitting at the counter, on the stool nearest the cash register.

The widow Palinkas turned away from the sink, a froth of soap on her hands. She could tell that Apostolos had been watching her. His eyes were full of lust as, smiling sheepishly, he pushed his empty coffee cup towards her.

"It's so late," she said in mock amazement. "Why don't you go home to bed, Apostolos?"

49

"It's lonely at home."

The widow Palinkas' eyes expressed grave concern. "Is your wife not at home?"

"Always." Apostolos smiled sadly. "Maybe that's why I'm so lonely. What do you think?"

Nichos, unable to hear what was said, strolled over to the counter too late to hear the punch line but just in time to join in the laughter. He put his capuccino cup down on the counter with a courtly, old-world gesture, and slapped his friend robustly on the shoulder.

"Come along, Apostolos. It's late, time to say good night."

Apostolos looked at the clock on the wall. He sighed heavily, pushed himself to his feet and gave Phasia Palinkas a regretful wave of his hand. "Until we meet again, dear lady."

Phasia Palinkas nodded, and suppressed a yawn.

At the door, Nichos stood to one side and waved Apostolos past him. When his friend was safely out on the sidewalk, Nichos turned and looked back at Phasia Palinkas. She was standing behind the cash register, her hands full of nickels and dimes and quarters.

"I'll see you tomorrow," said Nichos softly.

"No doubt." Her dark eyes were expressionless.

"Sooner, if you like."

She continued to count the coins, and the impressionable Nichos thought the sound of them clinking together must surely be the sound of his heart breaking apart under the strain of anticipated rejection. A strand of hair fell across her down-turned cheek. She brushed it away with the tips of her fingers, and at the same instant darted Nichos a sideways glance bursting with passion and heat.

He was electrified, struck dumb.

Phasia Palinkas forced herself to concentrate on the day's receipts. After a long moment, she heard the door shut, the click of the latch. She looked out the window and saw the two men crossing the street. Forcing the thought of Nichos' body from her mind, she went back to her counting. The sooner she was finished, the sooner she would be in her lover's arms.

As Nichos and Apostolos walked across the street towards

Culver's Sports Shop, Apostolos held his hand out palm up, as if he could not bring himself to believe that it had actually stopped raining. Then he blew the widow Palinkas a kiss she did not see, and laughed when Nichos punched him lightly on the shoulder. They paused for a moment in front of the store to discuss the merits of a new line of soccer balls displayed in the window. Above them, the hundreds of red and blue aluminium discs that formed the word CULVER's whirled and tinkled in the cold damp wind that swept down from the mountains.

As Nichos and Apostolos turned and began to walk down Commercial, Phasia Palinkas finally finished counting the day's take. There was more than a hundred and fifty dollars in her hands, the bills arranged according to denomination. She secured the money with a wide rubber-band and then shoved it in a canvas bank bag with a locking zipper. She put the bag in her purse, and then moved down the counter to the main electrical panel and switched off all the lights except the one by the rear door and the ceiling fixture over the cash register.

Having shrugged into her thick wool coat, she picked up her umbrella and went over to the door. She was about to leave when she noticed Nichos' capuccino cup on the counter. She walked back to the sink with it and ran a little cold water into it, to stop the sediment from congealing overnight.

Outside, she briskly rattled the door to test the lock.

A car raced past, stereo booming.

She clutched her purse tightly in her hands and began to walk rapidly down the cold, wind-swept street. The sidewalk was still wet from the rain. She could feel the chill seeping through the thin soles of her shoes. Her thoughts returned to Nichos, who by now must be waiting impatiently in the lobby of her apartment block. She and Nichos had been lovers two months now. He was very skilled, and despite the children in the adjoining bedroom, she was often noisier than she meant to be.

There was a sporty-looking little silver car parked in the middle of the block, and as she drew nearer she saw that it was a Mercedes. The windows of the car were fogged with condensation. As she walked past, she thought she noticed a vague movement behind the clouded glass.

Pressing her purse to her breast, she quickened her pace.

On the corner, no more than fifty feet away, there was a streetlight. Phasia Palinkas knew that once she stepped into that inviting pool of light, she would be safe. She tried to lengthen her stride, but the heavy wool coat made it difficult to hurry.

A sudden movement to her right startled her and she shied sideways, stumbled and almost fell. A face, eyes wide and mouth agape, peered out at her from the darkened window of a second-hand clothing store. She waved frantically. Her reflected image waved frantically back.

Behind her, the sniper stepped out of the Mercedes. The hem of his mauve vinyl raincoat caught on the doorhandle, and he yanked it free. Standing with one high-heeled shoe in the gutter and the other on the sidewalk, he carefully fitted a pair of fluffy pink earmuffs over his head. Then he put on the Bausch & Lomb glasses and reached behind him for the rifle.

It seemed to Phasia Palinkas that she had been fighting a treadmill, but finally she stepped out of the shadows and into the welcoming pool of light. Her panic had begun to subside. There were no footsteps behind her, and it had finally occurred to her that anyone who could afford a Mercedes would be unlikely to have much interest in her small bankroll. In fact she was beginning to wonder if she really had seen a movement inside the car, heard the soft click of a door opening behind her.

She glanced over her shoulder. Her breath caught in her throat as she saw a woman in a shiny plastic raincoat standing on the sidewalk next to the open door of the exotic little car. The woman's feet were wide apart and she seemed to be leaning slightly forward. Her right arm, elbow bent, was held out from her body parallel to the ground. Phasia Palinkas squinted into the gloom, and realized with a shock of horror that the woman was pointing a gun at her. Her heart thumped in her chest, spewing an adrenalin-rich mix of blood through her veins. She lurched into the centre of the puddle of light, and stood stock still.

The protection offered by the streetlight had been nothing but an illusion, no more substantial than a painted scrim.

A bright disc of light winked at her, reflected from the lens of the telescopic sight.

The sniper peered through the scope into a field of blackness irregularly sprinkled with a dozen tiny pinpoints of iridescence. Frowning, he moved the barrel laterally. The lens filled with light. In the lower left-hand quadrant there was a fuzzy black slope; the material, twice magnified, of Phasia Palinkas' black cloth coat. The iridescence, he saw now, had come from the many loose filaments of wool standing out from the mass. He tracked across the width of her shoulders, gauged the span, and tracked halfway back. The viewfinder was filled once again with blackness. He was, in a sense, shooting blind.

His finger tightened on the trigger.

Once again, the lens suddenly filled with light. He blinked. The crosshairs were focused on the shiny green metal of the lamp-post. It was as if he was looking at a slide show which made no sense and over which he had no control. He looked up, perplexed, and saw that Phasia Palinkas had moved and that she was in full flight.

He tried a snap shot, firing from the hip.

The bullet slammed into the small of her back. It threw her forward and knocked her down. Her head hit the sidewalk hard enough to fracture her cheekbone. She lay on her side on the cold wet concrete with one arm trapped beneath her and the other fully extended. The sound of the shot echoed down the length of the street, marching inexorably away from her.

Dimly, as if from a great distance, she heard the door of the Mercedes slam shut.

She opened her eyes. Her purse had burst open, spilling the contents across the sidewalk. Blurred scraps of paper drifted across her line of vision, past her key ring, a yellow nylon comb that belonged to her younger daughter, a scattered handful of coins that gleamed under the light.

The Mercedes coughed into life. She listened carefully, straining, as the muted clatter of the diesel engine faded to a perfect silence.

Everything kept shifting out of focus, sliding away from her. Suddenly the keys and comb and small change and the meaningless scraps of paper became enormously important. She was determined to retrieve them, to tidy up this last small segment of her life. Her fingers scrabbled spasmodically on the roughly textured surface of the sidewalk. A nail splintered. Minute laminations of polish crumbled and fell away along the irregular edge of the fracture. Never had her perspective been so small, details so significant. She stared at her hand as it staggered sideways of its own volition. The tendons in her wrist bulged. The fingers were arched and rigid. She watched the maverick hand march out of her line of sight and back again, pause six inches from her nose with the index finger flexed in mid-stride.

The air filled with mist. It began to rain. The streetlight above Phasia Palinkas retreated into a thick grey haze, slowly faded to black.

Nichos was in the lobby of Phasia Palinkas' apartment building when the fatal shot was fired. He was leaning against the steam radiator, idly running his fingers over the dusty leaves of an artificial rubber plant. As the blast of the sniper's rifle echoed down the street, he hurried to the double glass doors, and outside, into the rain. A silver Mercedes 450SL turned off Commercial and raced past him down Eleventh, headed west.

At the corner, Phasia Palinkas in her heavy black coat lay under the streetlight like a crumpled three-dimensional shadow. Nichos started slowly towards her, hesitated, broke into a trot. When he reached the body he skidded to a stop, fell to his knees. Her eyes stared through him. Rain streamed down her cheeks and into her open mouth, overflowed down her chin. A pool of blood seeped from beneath her, crawled slowly across the sidewalk towards him.

Nichos stole a quarter from the sidewalk. He looked around and saw no one, and hurried towards the pay phone at the far end of the block.

The sniper abandoned the silver 450SL in the public parking lot across from the tennis courts near the Beach Avenue entrance to Stanley Park. It was more than half a mile to the highrise on Jervis, and he had not thought to bring an umbrella. Within seconds of leaving the car, his cheap wig was plastered to his skull and his face was a ruin. But the driving rain that had reduced his disguise to an absurdity had also emptied the streets of pedestrians. Even Denman Street was deserted, except for a quartet of late-night diners clustered in the doorway of the Three Greenhorns restaurant. The sniper averted his face as he hurried past them, but no one paid any attention to him; it was as if he didn't exist.

It took him a quarter of an hour to make the trip from the Mercedes to his building. He turned his key in the lock and let himself into the lobby, which was small and bare, devoid of furniture. He punched the UP button. The doors to both elevators slid open simultaneously. He stepped into the closest elevator and hit the button for the twelfth floor. It was the last thrill of the night, this bold and risky ascent. But the elevator rose smoothly and without interruption. He saw no one, and no one saw him.

As he walked silently down the carpeted hallway towards his apartment, the sniper unbuttoned his mauve raincoat. The leather gun case hung straight down, suspended by a padded leather strap around his neck. He unlocked the door, went inside.

There was a tiny closet in the short entrance hall leading to the living room. The sniper pushed aside the flimsy louvred door and hung up his raincoat. Then he unhooked the padded strap and carried the rifle over to the pine table. Kicking off his high-heeled shoes, he reached awkwardly behind him to unzip the dress. The thin material was sopping wet. It clung tenaciously to him as he pulled the dress down to his hips. He wriggled free and let it fall in an untidy heap to the floor. Then he pulled off the blonde wig and tossed it underhand into the sink.

He was cold and he was wet, and he badly wanted a shower. But before he cleaned himself, he would clean the rifle.

Naked, shivering, he sat down on the bright orange plastic chair and went to work.

VI

A WHISTLE BLEW shrilly — one long, sharp note. The roar and clatter of power tools and hydraulic machinery stopped instantly, with all the precision of a superbly rehearsed symphony.

Bradley stood at his office window, looking down. He calculated that if the construction crew below him continued working at the same rate throughout the rest of the day, they would finish clearing the site by the end of the afternoon. That meant they could begin excavating first thing the following morning. Then, he knew, the level of noise would be truly horrendous. Sighing inwardly, he drank the rest of his lukewarm tea, put the Royal Albert gently down on the windowsill, and turned to face his two teams of detectives.

Claire Parker sat on one of the straight-backed wooden chairs, her hands resting quietly in her lap. Willows had assumed his customary position, against the wall within arm's reach of the door. Atkinson and Franklin were standing beside the cherry-wood desk. Atkinson's small, professionally manicured hands moved graphically as he continued to describe the previous evening's entanglements with Lynda, the skinny redhead from the cafeteria. Franklin had correctly guessed that his partner's ostentatious parading of the feathers was aimed at Claire Parker. Embarrassed, he kept glancing over at her while at the same time carefully avoiding eye contact. Franklin was fifty-two years old and known far and wide as a happily married man, but he thought he knew how Atkinson felt. No one in his right mind would deny that Parker was an extremely attractive woman. And despite the inclement weather, it was spring, that time of year when the saps begin to glow.

Bradley looked at his watch; a cheap Timex given to him by his twelve-year-old son, Christopher. It was two minutes past ten. Jerry Goldstein, who toiled in the bowels of the crime lab, over

56

on Grant and Keefer, was late again. Bradley twisted the ruby ring on the little finger of his left hand. He was a punctual man and punctuality was a trait he admired in others. He snuck another look at the scuffed crystal of the watch. Three minutes past ten, and counting. Bradley went over to his desk and sat down. "What time you got?" he said to Dave Atkinson.

Atkinson knew exactly what was on Bradley's mind. "Five past," he lied.

Bradley opened his carved cedar humidor and helped himself to a cigar. He'd been smoking more heavily since the death of Alice Palm, and he didn't like it one little bit. He was going to have to make an effort to cut back, and not just for the sake of his health. The cigars were costly as hell. Like most cops, he was on a budget.

He struck a wooden kitchen match against the belly of his desk, let the flame settle, and lit up. A cloud of aromatic Cuban smoke billowed towards the ceiling, nine feet high and splattered here and there with dark, oddly shaped stains.

The feeling of intense irritation caused by Goldstein's tardiness refused to abate. Bradley glared at the Timex. It was what, about six minutes past ten, and he was already smoking his afternoon cigar — a cigar that had cost him a dollar fifty and wasn't giving him a nickel's worth of pleasure. Sitting bolt upright in his leather chair, he continued to stare menacingly at the watch, his eyes on the sweep second hand as it dragged slowly around the dial.

At ten minutes past the hour, just as the construction whistle signalled an end to the morning coffee break, Jerry Goldstein finally waltzed into the office.

"Sorry I'm late," said Goldstein to the room at large. "It was unavoidable. A lady down on the second floor had a seizure, and I had to help regurgitate her tongue."

"Life and death," said Bradley. "I figured it had to be something like that."

Goldstein nodded, ignoring Bradley's tone. Goldstein was wearing a lightweight cream-coloured three-piece suit, a chocolate brown Italian silk tie and an impossibly white silk shirt. His shoes were made of canvas the exact same shade of brown as his tie, and had thick soles and heels of translucent pink plastic. His socks, also of chocolate brown silk, sported a pattern of yellow sundials. He gave Parker a lazy smile.

"You must be the new crime-buster."

"Claire Parker."

"Jerry Goldstein." Goldstein smiled again, his eyes twinkling. Thanks to his tinted contact lenses, his eyes were almost as blue as Paul Newman's. His teeth were large, as white as his impossibly white shirt. Jumbled together in cramped and disorderly rows, they gave him a charming, almost piratical air. With his flash clothes, the eyes, his full head of curly blond hair and cherubic complexion, Goldstein knew he looked good. He also knew it was no time to flirt, not with Bradley sitting there behind a cloud of smoke that might or might not be coming from his cigar.

Without preamble, he began his lecture.

"The earmuffs that were found on the sidewalk down the street from the pool hall were probably used by the shooter to protect himself from the sound of the shot. We tracked down the manufacturer. The muffs are carried by three department store chains and dozens of independents. More than six thousand pairs have been sold in and around the city in the past two years."

"Maybe so," said Atkinson. "But how many of them were pink?"

"About half. They only come in two colours. Blue for boys, pink for girls."

"Naturally," said Parker.

"What's the matter," said Goldstein, "you don't like pink?"

"Only in sunsets. What about the spent cartridge that was found in the Mercedes?"

"No doubt about it, it definitely came from the same weapon that was used on Alice Palm."

"Hold it," said Franklin. "What Mercedes?"

"A 450SL," said Bradley. "The owner's name is Douglas Phillips. He reported the vehicle stolen at 8:07 this morning."

"When was it recovered?"

"At 7:12, almost an hour before the switchboard logged Phillip's call. The car was left with the lights on and both doors wide open. A squad car came across it during a routine patrol. The cops took a look inside, saw the spent cartridge on the floor, and gave me a call."

"Anybody talk to Phillips yet?"

"I did," said Parker. "His wife's a light sleeper. She says she was with him all night long."

"Has he got any other character witnesses, other than his wife?" said Atkinson.

Parker nodded. "His doctor. Phillips has a long history of heart trouble."

"Well," said Atkinson, "I can certainly relate to that."

"The man had a near-fatal stroke two years ago," Parker continued. "A pacemaker was implanted, but even so, he has to be very careful. Any degree of stress or excitement would be extremely risky."

"The guy wears a pacemaker *and* he's married?" Atkinson winked broadly at Franklin. "What do they call that, George, double indemnity?"

"Other than the cartridge," said Willows, "was there anything inside the car?"

"It was in what you might call absolutely showroom condition," said Goldstein. "Except for one small detail."

"And what was that?" said Bradley, who strongly resented Goldstein's habit of doling out scraps and fragments of information as if he was doing volunteer work in a soup kitchen, expertly feeding his captive audience just enough to keep them balanced on the knife edge of starvation.

"The ashtray," said Goldstein, "was jammed with half-smoked cigarette butts." He turned to Parker. "The guy's wife, does she smoke?"

"I didn't ask. But I didn't see any ashtrays in the house, and she didn't smoke during the time I was there."

"And Phillips wouldn't smoke because he's got a bad heart," said Franklin.

"Besides," said Goldstein, "he probably doesn't wear lipstick."

"Lipstick?" said Bradley.

"Yeah, right. Lipstick." Goldstein unbuttoned his suit jacket and thrust his hands deep into his trouser pockets. "You got a witness says he saw a woman driving away from the Alice Palm murder, isn't that right?"

"Shelley Rice," said Bradley.

"Any sign of that car yet?"

"No," said Bradley shortly. He made a pass with his cigar over the wastebasket. "Any more tidbits for us, Jerry?"

"Nope, you squeezed me dry."

"Well listen, you've been a wonderful guest, and I want you to come back real soon."

"Call me day or night," said Goldstein, talking to Bradley but looking at Parker.

Bradley made a tent of his fingers and played spider on a mirror until Goldstein had made his exit.

"You catch those shoes?" said Atkinson. "See-through soles, real trendy."

Bradley laced his fingers together, making a double fist. "You check the sporting goods store across the street from where the Palinkas woman was shot?" he said to Franklin.

Franklin nodded. He made a move for his notebook and then decided he didn't need it. "The owner's name is Morris Culver. He and his wife live in a little apartment at the back of the store. Dave and I went over there first thing this morning, caught them going out the door."

"On their way to church," said Atkinson. "All dressed up in their Sunday best."

"To confess?"

"Not to murder."

"Culver's been in business a long time," said Franklin, "close to thirty years. He's stayed in the black by keeping his stock levels low, pushing whatever happens to be in season. Baseball, hockey, all that stuff. But most of his income the past ten years has been generated by the sale of firearms and reloading equipment."

Bradley's head came up. "Tell me more, George."

"Culver's wife keeps the company books. According to her records, they sold a special order of two hundred rounds of .460 Magnum bullets and brass three months ago, on January 4th, to a woman named Lilly Watts."

60

"They have an address?"

"Apartment five-seventeen, the Manhattan. That's a co-op on the corner of Robson and Thurlow. There's some shops on the ground floor, a travel agency, bookstore, a restaurant."

"Binky's," said Atkinson. "Best clam chowder in town."

"Let's wait until we solve the case," said Bradley. "Then we can have lunch."

"We went down there and had a look around," Franklin said. "No such apartment. No such tenant."

"Lilly also left a phone number at Culver's. We gave her a ring and got a time-of-day message." Atkinson grinned. "More than most crooks will give you."

"Was Culver able to come up with a description?" said Parker.

"Afraid not," said Franklin. "He's half-blind without his glasses, and he hardly ever wears them because one of the little plastic nosepads fell off, and they pinch. But he does remember that Lilly Watts was a blonde, and that she was unusually tall."

"How tall is that?" said Willows.

"Taller than Culver," said Franklin. And then added, "Who was, I'd say, about five foot seven."

"The same height as Dave," said Willows.

"I'm five-ten," said Atkinson, flushing angrily.

"Shoes by Otis," said Willows.

Bradley pulled on his cigar but got no smoke. He struck a match against his thumbnail, fired up, and waved the match at Willows. "Jack, I want you and Parker to concentrate on Alice Palm. Dig into her background, and dig deep. We still don't know where she was going when she was killed, and she's been dead eight days now."

The match was still burning. Bradley remembered a scene in *Lawrence of Arabia*, Peter O'Toole extinguishing a match with his fingers and saying something about it being an easy trick to learn, all you had to do was not show the pain. He dropped the spent match in the wastebasket, and turned his attention to Atkinson.

"Dave, you and George find out everything there is to know about Phasia Palinkas. If there's any kind of connection between the two victims, I want to know about it." Bradley blew a fat

61

doughnut of smoke across the surface of his desk. He pointed at the doughnut with the stub of his cigar. "That's exactly what we've got so far. Zilch. A big fat zero. It ain't good enough."

Willows started to move towards the door. Bradley held up a restraining hand.

"One more thing. I got a phone call from Chief Scott this morning. Early this morning. He'd been talking to Mayor Cooley, who strongly resents the fact that two of this fair city's voters have been so spectacularly whacked. The headlines, as you may have noticed, have not been kind. His Honour wants the perp disenfranchised with all due haste, before he decides to try for three in a row. So let's find the son of a bitch and put him down, okay?"

As they left Bradley's office, Willows touched Parker's arm and said, "I've got to make a call. I'll meet you in the parking lot in ten minutes."

Parker nodded, but Willows had already slipped past her, left her behind.

It had been three days since Willows' last visit to the cancer ward of the Royal Columbian, and it was past time he gave the hospital a call. There was an enclosed payphone in the hallway next to the service elevator used to transport prisoners to the holding cells and drunk tank on the third floor. The booth was empty. Willows went inside and pushed the folding glass doors shut behind him. The automatic light came on and he saw that the telephone's receiver had been ripped out of the body of the instrument. The receiver lay on the floor of the booth, next to a shredded copy of the yellow pages. Someone had got it wrong, and taken his fist for a walk. Willows stepped out of the booth. He heard the slow clanking of the service elevator ascending, and pushed the UP button. There was another payphone on the third floor, installed there for the convenience of those crooks and drunkards who wanted to call a bondsman or family, to make bail, or excuses.

He heard the elevator slow down, stop. There was a pause, and then the doors jerked open. Willows walked into the elevator and found himself standing face to face with Shelley Rice.

Rice was flanked by a couple of chunky six-footers from Narcotics, Ralph Kearns and Eddy Orwell. Rice's eyes darkened as he recognized Willows. He shifted his weight, and the steel on his wrists glinted under the harsh light from the quartet of naked hundred-watt bulbs in the ceiling fixture.

"I'd introduce you two guys to each other," said Orwell, grinning, "but I believe you've already met."

"They busted you?" Willows said to Rice.

Rice's face contorted with rage. He lunged forward, his knee coming up hard and fast. Willows twisted sideways. The knee hit him in the thigh, right on the bone. He grunted with pain. An elbow caught him flush on the nose. The back of his head bounced off the sheet metal wall of the elevator. He staggered into Kearns, who went down. Willows fought to regain his balance. Orwell was cursing imaginatively, fumbling under his coat for a sap or his gun. Rice clasped his manacled hands together and raised them high over his head. The four lightbulbs exploded in a shower of glass. For a fraction of a second the filaments glowed like a handful of incandescent worms, then the elevator was plunged into absolute darkness.

Willows heard the sharp metallic click of a revolver being cocked. Instinctively, he went for his own weapon. The elevator jerked to a stop. The doors slid open and the elevator was filled with light. Orwell was pointing his gun at Kearns. Willows lashed out. His fist thudded into Rice's stomach, and Rice sighed wistfully, and doubled over. Willows resisted the urge to hit him again. There was something warm and wet on his upper lip. His nose was bleeding. He yanked a pale green handkerchief from the breast pocket of Rice's jacket, and pressed it against the flow.

"Will you put that thing away?" said Kearns.

Orwell holstered his gun.

The doors started to slide shut. Willows stopped them with his foot. He gingerly wiped his nose. There was lace on the handkerchief. He took a closer look, and saw that he had wiped his nose with a pair of panties. He dropped the bloodstained panties to the floor.

"You okay?" said Orwell.

"He didn't break it, if that's what you're asking."

"Man, you sure congeal fast. Means you got a lot of red blood cells, that you must be eating right."

Shelley Rice was still bent double, looking a little like a failed comedian taking an undeserved bow. Willows grabbed him by the lapels, pulled him upright and held him against the wall of the elevator.

"Why did you hit me?"

"What the fuck do you think?"

"I don't know what to think," said Willows. "That's why I asked you."

"You gave me your word you weren't interested in dope, and then you turned me over to the narcs."

"I don't know what you're talking about."

"Then what are you doing here, asshole?"

"Watch your mouth," said Kearns, and punched Rice in the kidneys.

"Hey," said Willows. "Don't do that again."

"First it's your nose that's bleeding," said Kearns. "Now it's your heart."

Willows turned to Orwell. "What have you got on him?"

"Coke, about fifty grams. Possession with intent. Not exactly the crime of the century, but enough to make his parole officer do some heavy thinking."

"Who turned him in?"

"You're asking me?" said Orwell, looking surprised.

Kearns was making a noise like somebody shaking a tin can full of rocks. Willows looked at him, and saw that he was laughing.

The phone rang eleven times before the hospital switchboard answered. By then Willows had figured out that it had to be Claire Parker who'd turned Rice over to Orwell and Kearns. A gift bust was always good for interdepartmental points, future cooperation from the beneficiaries. But it wasn't the way Willows liked to play the game. Worse, he was sure that Parker had heard him promise Rice they weren't interested in the fact that he was dealing.

No doubt about it, Parker had made a mistake. The question was, what was Willows going to do about it?

VII

ATKINSON STRAIGHT-ARMED his way past the bevelled glass doors and into the lobby. A mock-bamboo stand full of dusty plastic plants stood beside the steam radiator. He ran his fingers across a broad green leaf, and it fell away from the main stem and spiralled to the carpet. Unbuttoning his raincoat, Atkinson kicked the leaf under the radiator. Behind him, Franklin hurried up the short sidewalk from Eleventh Avenue. Pushing his way through the glass doors, he stamped his feet and shook the rain from his hat.

Directly in front of them a narrow carpeted hallway ran the length of the building, twin rows of polished brass doorknobs shrinking into the distance. To the left a staircase led to the second and third floors. Atkinson started up the stairs, taking them two at a time, always in a hurry. Franklin followed at a more sedate pace, but by the time he reached the second-floor landing he was having trouble with his wind. He paused with his hand on the railing, his chest heaving. The unending overtime, junk food, constant pressure — they were all part of the job and they all conspired against good health. And he had to admit he wasn't getting any younger. There was that. Glancing up, Franklin saw Atkinson looking at him with what might almost have passed for an expression of sympathy. It made him feel even worse.

Atkinson was standing on the second-floor landing, next to a child's bicycle that was chained to the banister. Someone not too handy with a brush had painted the bicycle midnight blue. The seat had been patched with electrician's tape. A squat and badly rusted bell was fastened to the butterfly handlebars. Atkinson rang the bell twice as he walked past the bike, as if signalling an official end to Franklin's rest period.

Franklin had his hand on the newel post at the turn of the stairs when the apartment door closest to the landing swung open. He and Atkinson both turned as a young Chinese woman, a sleeping infant in her arms, stepped silently into the hall. Atkinson paused. He stared at the woman, making no pretext of waiting for Franklin to catch up. The woman was no more than eighteen or nineteen years old. She was tall and slim, and wore a colourful orange and red cotton skirt and a thin black turtleneck sweater. Her long black hair fell in a heavy mass to her narrow waist, fanned artfully around the gentle swell of her hips. Moving lightly and gracefully despite the burden of the child, the woman turned and shut the door.

Atkinson watched her, his eyes busy on the round fullness of her breasts as she turned her key in the lock, tested the door to make sure it was secure. As she moved towards the stairs, he tried without success to catch her eye. Using the banister for support, he leaned far out over the stairs to watch her descend. She glanced up, pursed her lips in disapproval, and looked away.

The two detectives walked down the landing and began to climb the final flight of stairs. Despite the short respite offered by the landing, Franklin once again found himself running short of wind. He loosened his tie and slipped the top button of his shirt. Atkinson grinned at him. He had a one-step advantage, but their eyes were almost level.

"She really started the old heart pumping, eh George?"

"What's that?"

"Got a thing about Oriental girls?"

Franklin shook his head. "Give it a rest, Dave." He took out his handkerchief and pushed back his hat to wipe his forehead.

Atkinson laughed harshly. "It doesn't need a rest," he said, "it needs all the exercise it can get."

Franklin looked down at his handkerchief, carefully refolded it and tucked it away in his pocket. Atkinson was thirty-seven years old and he was smirking like a schoolboy. Unbelievable. Franklin brushed past his partner, taking the steps one at a time, pacing himself.

At the top of the stairs there was another long and narrow hallway. At the end of the hallway a window had been propped open with a hockey stick. The breeze coming in through the

66

window was sweet and cool. Franklin took several deep breaths, gulping it in. Feeling a little refreshed, he followed Atkinson down the hallway, past a series of identical anonymous doors.

Phasia Palinkas' apartment was the last one on the left. Atkinson took a key ring out of his pocket. There were seven keys on the ring. The third one he tried slipped easily into the lock. He pushed the door open and they went inside.

The front door opened directly on to the living room. The room was small, and not quite a perfect square. It was furnished with a cheap two-piece Chesterfield suite in a blue floral pattern, a pair of mismatched veneer coffee tables and a portable colour television. Against the far wall there was an antique gas fire made of cast-iron and chromed steel. Franklin went over to it and turned it on. He heard the hiss of escaping gas.

"You better turn that off," said Atkinson.

Franklin struck a paper match, and the gas caught with a soft *whuff*. Franklin lit a cigarette, warmed his hands at the flames. Steam drifted from his raincoat and the brim of his hat. He closed his eyes.

"Hey," said Atkinson. "Rise and shine. You forget Bradley's pep talk already? Let's get to work."

Atkinson pushed open a pair of sliding wooden doors and walked through to the dining room. The room was sparsely furnished. There was a chrome and formica table, four matching chairs, an oak sideboard that had seen better days. Atkinson opened the top drawer of the sideboard and began to shuffle through the contents.

Franklin reluctantly left the fire and followed his partner into the dining room. He looked out of the window at the stucco wall of the neighbouring apartment, less than ten feet away. The wall was made of white stucco that had turned green with mildew. In the narrow space between the two buildings an abandoned refrigerator lay on its back in the weeds and grass. It was still raining.

Franklin yawned, covering his mouth with the back of his hand. Behind him, Atkinson slid the drawer shut and opened another one. Paper rustled in his hands.

And there was another sound, too, a thick and mucous bubbling. Franklin drew his revolver. Atkinson looked at him, surprised. Franklin put a finger to his lips and pointed at the swing door at the far end of the room. Atkinson dropped a handful of cancelled cheques, reached under his jacket and pulled his Colt. The two detectives converged on the door from opposite sides of the formica table. Atkinson pressed his ear against the wood. There was a sound coming from the far side of the door that was exactly the same as a sound he had heard five years earlier, in a warehouse doorway on the fringe of Chinatown. The sound had come from the red froth of a throat that had been slashed from ear to ear. The body had never been identified, and neither had the cutter. He was still out there, somewhere.

Atkinson renewed his grip on the Colt. He took a half-step back and then lunged forward, giving the door such a ferocious kick that the bottom hinge tore loose from the frame. There was a high-pitched scream of bent metal and splintering wood. The door flew open, gouging a pale scar across green linoleum.

Franklin was first through the door, first into the kitchen. Following the sound to its source, he saw a piece of three-quarter-inch plywood spiked to the sill of a double hung window overlooking the parking lot and lane at the rear of the building. The plywood supported a rectangular ten-gallon fish tank inhabited by three plump goldfish. The fish hovered just below the surface of the water, motionless except for the gauzy shimmering of pectoral fins, the occasional flick of a tail.

There was a small electric pump hanging from a hook screwed into the plywood. From the pump a length of flexible plastic tubing led to a clear plastic box half-buried in the brightly col- oured gravel that covered the bottom of the tank. The box was full of charcoal. Air pumped through the tubing was purified by the charcoal and then released, the endless cloud of tiny silver bubbles oxygenating the water as they rose to the surface and burst. This was the source of the sound that had reminded Atkin- son of the man in Chinatown, the man with the big red grin.

"Shit," said Atkinson. His shoulders sagged. He stared out the window, down at the parking lot. There was a fourteen-foot Peterborough on a trailer in the corner stall. A rusty thirty-five horse Johnson outboard motor hung disconsolately from the stern. The boat was carrying five or six inches of oily water; the iridescent surface pocked with rain.

Atkinson suddenly felt hot, feverish. He was afraid that he was going to be ill. He went over to the sink and ran the cold water. As he bent to drink, he saw that someone had dropped a jar of strawberry jam on the counter next to the dishrack. The glass jar had shattered, the bright red jam spreading across the counter like an exotic, morbid flower. He picked up a shard of glass, put it back.

Franklin leaned over Atkinson's shoulder and stuck his finger in the jam. It felt hard and rubbery, a bit like Silly Putty. He pushed harder. His finger broke through the exterior film and sank into the oozy mass right up to the middle joint.

Franklin pulled out the dripping finger and plunged it into his mouth.

Atkinson looked wildly around. He crossed rapidly to the pump, reached down and yanked the electric cord out of the socket. The sound of the pump and bubbling water abruptly died away.

"Something wrong?" said Franklin, licking the last of the jam from his finger.

Atkinson shrugged irritably, not looking up from the tank. The three goldfish shifted laterally in unison, adjusting to the diminishing currents. He tapped the barrel of his gun against the glass and the fish panicked, darting off in different directions. Atkinson watched with a curious sense of satisfaction as they swam frantically and aimlessly about. After a few moments the fish regrouped, huddling closely together in the middle of the tank with their sleek bellies brushing against the gravel bottom.

Atkinson gave the tank another whack with his gun. The glass cracked diagonally from the bottom left to the top right corner. The fish bolted again, but with less enthusiasm. Atkinson wondered if they were tiring or merely adapting. Halfway along the crack a bead of water wriggled free, paused, and then dribbled hesitantly down to the plywood shelf. A second drop of water appeared, and then a third. The largest of the fish swam circuitously over to investigate. It followed the next droplet down the side of the tank, its round mouth opening and closing rhythmically. It must be hungry, Atkinson thought. He glanced up and saw Franklin staring at him, a quizzical expression on his bland and ponderous face.

The drops were coming more quickly now. They gathered on the lip of the plywood, fell in a thin stream to the linoleum floor.

Atkinson said, "You like fish, George?"

"Not much. When I was a kid we had to eat fish every Friday. You ever tried week after week of tuna picnic loaf and festive haddock fillets?"

"I'm talking about salmon, not fucking haddock. Thick slices of coho with lemon, a sprig of parsley on the side."

"Parsley?"

"Always eat your parsley, George. If you're in a restaurant and they don't give you any, ask for it. You can't find a better source of vitamin C."

"If you say so," said Franklin, his eyes fixed on the spreading puddle on the linoleum.

"All seafood is good for you," Atkinson continued. "It's packed with protein and low in fat content. Also, the oceans are relatively free of chemical fertilizers and insecticides, all that death shit your average Farmer Brown sprays all over his crops."

"Makes sense to me," said Franklin warily. There was no way he was going to argue with a guy who could pull the plug on an orphan's pet fish.

"You are what you eat," said Atkinson. "It's a cliché, but it's true." He brought up his Colt and scratched himself behind the ear with the blade of the revolver's front sight.

Franklin reached for the pack of cigarettes in his shirt pocket. He lit up, exhaled a cloud of carcinogens, flicked ash on the floor.

Atkinson led the way through another door to the narrow corridor that bisected the back half of the apartment. They were standing opposite the bathroom. Down the hall, open doors led to the apartment's two bedrooms. Atkinson went into the bathroom and switched on the light. He rummaged through the medicine cabinet until he found a slim plastic vial of aspirin. Running water from the sink into his cupped left hand, he popped two of the tablets into his mouth, and swallowed.

70

Neither Atkinson nor Franklin seemed to notice the fourth goldfish as it floated on its side in the toilet bowl, one eye dangling at the end of a scarlet thread.

The first bedroom had obviously been Phasia Palinkas'. There was a big mahogany bed, an oak bow-front bureau with an oval bevelled glass mirror, and a writing desk where she had worked on her business accounts. To the left of the door there was a walk-in closet. Atkinson went into the closet, and Franklin heard the rattle of metal coat-hangers. He blew a plume of smoke into the air, stared thoughtfully down at the scuffed toes of his shoes. Five minutes with a brush and rag, that was all they needed. A dab of polish and they'd look as if they'd just come out of the box. The coat-hangers rattled again. Atkinson came out of the closet. He plucked a speck of lint from his lapel, scrutinized the bedroom with an expert's eye. Something on the desk caught his attention. He went over to the desk and picked up the phone. The cord had been ripped from the wall. "I wonder how this happened," he said.

"I can tell you always pay your bills on time," joked Franklin.

Atkinson looped the cord around the phone and tossed the phone on the bed. A spring creaked. Atkinson walked over to the bureau and pulled open the top drawer. Several bundles of letters, each neatly tied with a pink ribbon, lay beside the folded piles of Phasia Palinkas' sturdy underwear. Atkinson holstered the Colt and picked up one of the bundles. The Greek stamps were ornate, sombre. "Why don't you go take a look in the other bedroom?" Atkinson said to Franklin.

Franklin hesitated, and then nodded.

Atkinson picked at the tight knot of the ribbon. He was hardly aware that Franklin had left the room until the stillness of the apartment was shattered by the insane mechanical quacking of a toy duck. He glanced up, startled, and then realized the sound was coming from the children's room. He returned his attention to the ribbon, and at that exact instant, as if by magic, the knot came undone. Atkinson opened the topmost envelope and unfolded the sheets of flimsy, yellowed paper.

The letter was written in Greek.

Atkinson was stuffing the letter back in the envelope when a small black and white photograph slipped from between the pages and into the open drawer. The photograph was of Phasia Palinkas, aged sixteen. She was standing in front of a squat white house with a flat roof and thick plaster walls. The windows were shuttered against the heat of the sun. An old woman dressed all in black sat on a wooden stool in the deep shadow of the doorway.

The photographer had adjusted the aperture and shutter speed of his camera correctly to expose his subject's skin tone. Because of this the background was badly over-exposed, bleached an almost featureless white except for the old woman and a rhomboid of pale grey in the upper left-hand corner. Atkinson studied this unlikely shape. Finally he decided it was nothing but a slice of thin air wedged between the house and a neighbouring building, slightly distorted by the camera's lens.

A gust of wind made the bedroom window rattle in its frame. Rain danced across the glass. Atkinson rubbed the back of his neck.

Phasia Palinkas, aged sixteen, had posed with her hands clasped modestly in front of her, all but lost in the voluminous folds of her long black skirt. She was wearing a loose white blouse with puff sleeves. At her throat a chip of metal glinted brightly in the sun. A wealth of straight black hair cascaded from her shoulders to her breasts, artfully defined by the accidental pattern of light and shadow. Her face was heart-shaped — wide cheekbones above a firm but gently rounded chin. Dark eyebrows gave balance to her prominent nose. Her mouth was full, the lips slightly parted.

There was strength in that small, carefully composed face, and a quality of innocence that Atkinson found intriguing. He stared down at the girl's image, an image seen through the translucent summer air of Greece, a lifetime of lost and irretrievable years. And perhaps because he had nothing to lose, he allowed himself to be touched.

A sharp movement in the bureau's oval mirror distracted him from his reverie. He saw the barrel of a rifle sweep across the silvered glass, heard the soft click of a released safety-catch. His stomach muscles contracted. He twisted clumsily around, his hand clawing at his Colt.

In the other bedroom, the mechanical duck howled with laughter.

Atkinson cried out, but his words were drowned in the enormous roar of the .460 Magnum.

He watched the photograph of Phasia Palinkas flutter lazily through the air and come to rest on the carpet near his feet. He had ended up, somehow, sitting on the floor with his back against the footboard of the bed.

His body was numb. There was no pain, not yet. He peered down at his spotless white shirt and saw a spreading red stain. He'd been gutshot, hit low. The red stain was creeping up the front of his shirt, crawling swiftly across his belly towards his chest. Fucking osmosis. There was a lot of blood on his pants, too. And his jacket. He was going to have a hell of a dry-cleaning bill. He tried to laugh. His mouth gaped open and his upper plate fell out. A rope of saliva trailed from his chin.

On the far side of the room, the window slid open. He felt a wash of cold air across his face. The room vibrated with a flurry of shots.

To Atkinson, they seemed impossibly far away.

VIII

ATKINSON SEEMED TO have reacted to death by physically shrinking away from it, so that he appeared even smaller now than he had been in life. Despite the crisp white shirt, expensive tailored suit and new Hart shoes, his corpse somehow managed to look ill-dressed.

Willows put the snapshot of Phasia Palinkas down on the bureau, and crouched beside the body. The toe of his brogue rested less than an inch from the kidney-shaped pool of blood that continued, almost an hour after the shoot, to leak from the terrible excavation in the dead man's body. Willows was acutely aware of the steady thud of blood dripping on the sodden carpet, in time with the slow beating of his heart.

Behind Willows, a detective named Farley Spears leaned out of the bedroom window, his face tilted to the rain.

As he had exited the sniper had pushed the window frame up as far as it would go, creating a gap roughly twenty inches wide by eighteen inches high. Franklin's first three rounds had punctured the glass. There were two more closely spaced holes in the frame. The bullets had splintered the wood, exposing several layers of paint — strata of green, yellow, turquoise and mauve. Spears thought that the multiple laminations of colour looked a little like a cross-section of an improperly constructed rainbow. The thought cheered him. He turned around, and covertly stared at Franklin.

Franklin sat on the edge of the big mahogany bed. Claire Parker sat next to him. The simple act of witnessing Franklin's grief had left her feeling empty, exhausted. For half an hour or more Franklin had rocked gently back and forth, hugging himself, the tears streaming down his cheeks. Every few minutes an unnerving high-pitched whine of despair had escaped from between his clenched teeth. Parker had hugged him and held him

74

and never stopped talking to him, using her voice as a sedative. Franklin had gradually managed to bring himself under control. Now he was just sitting there, drained, motionless.

Parker glanced up as the cop slouching at the door suddenly pulled himself erect.

A moment later Bradley came into the room, an unlit cigar in one hand and a match in the other. He stared impassively down at Atkinson's corpse and then struck the match viciously against the side of the bureau. When he had the cigar burning to his satisfaction he looked up from Atkinson's body and nodded tersely at his four detectives.

His eyes lingered on Parker. She looked pale, badly shaken. Give them too much meat, he thought, and they won't mouse. He put an expression of fatherly concern on his face, fitting it in around the cigar.

"You okay?"

"Fine," said Parker, rejecting the overture.

Bradley glanced at Franklin, at the bowed shoulders and the big wet face etched with tension and dismay. He went over to the body and hunkered down next to Willows.

"What happened, Jack?"

Willows shrugged. "Ask George."

"You haven't talked to him yet?"

"He wasn't ready." Atkinson was still dripping, but more slowly now. There were stalactites of dark congealing blood in the folds and creases of his trousers. His face was white. The eyes were dull, gelatinous, monumentally disinterested.

Bradley stirred as a tall, gaunt man with a grey pencil moustache came briskly into the room. He was carrying a black leather Gladstone bag, and he looked as if he wouldn't know what to do with himself if he wasn't in a hurry.

Bradley stood up, knees creaking. "Coroner's office?"

The man nodded. "Milne," he said. Frowning at Farley Spears, he said, "Would you mind closing that window?"

Spears shot Bradley an enquiring look, which Bradley blandly ignored. Spears shut the window.

Milne unbuttoned Atkinson's shirt and stuck a thermometer under his armpit. While he was waiting for the mercury to climb,

75

he took an eyedropper out of the black bag and dribbled a clear liquid on to Atkinson's eyes, then gently shut the lids.

Jerry Goldstein and a police photographer named Mel Dutton squeezed past the cop at the door. Goldstein was carrying a Heinkens portable fingerprint kit. Dutton had two Nikons and an old Speed Graphic slung around his neck. Behind them, two men wheeled a stretcher into the room. It was getting crowded, and it was getting hot.

"Would you open that window, Farley?" said Goldstein loudly.

Milne looked up, annoyed.

Bradley went over to the bed and touched Franklin on the shoulder. "Let's get out of here, George."

Franklin contemplated Bradley's splayed fingers, the bright red spark of his ruby ring. He blew into his handkerchief, scrubbed at his nose.

Bradley motioned Willows over. Together the two men helped Franklin to his feet and led him out of the room.

Mel Dutton began to circle the body in an artistic crouch, the power winder of his Nikon whirring and clicking as it pulled frame after frame of film through the spools. To Parker, sitting alone on the edge of the bed, it seemed as if the effect of the camera's electronic flash was to suck all the remaining traces of colour right out of Dave Atkinson's slack and pallid face.

Bradley waved his cigar at the bathroom door, and Willows pushed it shut with the flat of his hand. Franklin dropped the toilet lid and sat down heavily. Bradley perched on the rim of the big cast-iron bathtub. Willows went over to the sink and ran the cold water. He soaked one end of a threadbare orange towel and then handed the towel to Franklin.

"Wipe your face, George."

Franklin nodded, and methodically washed and dried his face.

"That feel better?" said Bradley.

"Sure," said Franklin affably.

Bradley chewed on his cigar, waiting for Franklin to get started. Franklin shut his eyes. "Why don't you tell us what happened?" Bradley said.

"Okay," said Franklin, opening his eyes. He wiped the back of his neck with the towel and then neatly folded it upon itself until it wouldn't fold any smaller. "I was in the other bedroom when I heard the shot," he finally said.

"In the kids' bedroom?" said Bradley, making sure he had it right.

"Yeah, in the kids' bedroom."

"What were you doing in there, George?"

"Playing."

Bradley glanced at Willows and then back at Franklin. "What's that again?"

"Playing. I was playing with a little yellow duck I found in there."

Bradley frowned down at Franklin through the smoke from his cigar.

"Maybe we ought to back up a little," suggested Willows.

Franklin shrugged. "Whatever you say."

"When you first entered the apartment," said Bradley, "did you lock the door after you?"

"Yeah, sure. Of course we did."

"Then the killer must've already been inside when you and Dave arrived on the scene."

"Well, yeah. The way I figure it, we must've taken him by surprise. Otherwise, why would he have shot Dave?"

"Where do you think he might have been hiding?" said Bradley.

Franklin thought about it at length, his eyes on the floor. "I got no idea," he said at last. "Between us, Dave and I went through every room in the place."

"What about the closets?" said Willows.

"There's only a couple in the apartment. One in the kitchen and another in the bedroom."

"You look inside?" said Bradley.

"The one in the kitchen had the door open when we were in there. As for the big walk-in closet in the bedroom, Dave was rummaging around in there for a couple of minutes at least."

"Doing what?"

"I don't know. Maybe looking for a little present for his girlfriend. A dress, blouse, whatever."

"You're kidding me."

"Not today," said Franklin.

The silence that followed was punctuated by the steady dripping of the cold water tap. Willows had recently heard that sound before. He leaned across Franklin and twisted the handle. A last drop trembled on the lip of the tap, and reluctantly fell.

"At what point did you and Dave split up?" said Bradley.

"Just before he got shot. A minute, maybe less. We were both in the bedroom, poking around. Dave got interested in some letters he found, and suggested I go take a look in the kids' room."

"You sure it was his idea to separate, George?"

Franklin nodded. "Yeah, I'm sure."

"Was that after he went through the clothes closet?"

"Had to be, didn't it." Franklin took out his pack of cigarettes and offered them around. Bradley held up his cigar. Willows politely declined; he hadn't smoked in five years. Franklin stuck a cigarette in his mouth and patted himself down in a futile search for a light. Bradley handed Franklin one of his big kitchen matches. Franklin struck the match against the heel of his shoe. The stench of burning sulphur soured the air.

"Tell us about the shoot," said Bradley.

Franklin inhaled deeply, exhaled slowly. "Like I said, I was in the other bedroom."

"Playing with a duck."

Franklin blew out the match and tossed it in the sink. "There was a whole bunch of toy animals lined up in a row on a shelf above the beds. And right at the end there was this little yellow duck with a key sticking out of its back. I picked it up and went over to the window, looked out at the rain. And without thinking about what I was doing, I wound that duck up good and tight and put it down on the windowsill. It started making this really weird sound, jumping around like it had pogo sticks for legs.

"I was trying to figure out if there was any way to turn it off when I heard the shot."

Franklin took a long pull on his cigarette. Smoke dribbled out of his nostrils, into his eyes.

"I shouted Dave's name, but I didn't get a response. The duck was making a hell of a racket. I pulled my gun and ran back into the other bedroom.

"Dave was lying on his back on the floor. His arms were at his sides. He was looking down at his stomach, all that blood. He had a look in his eyes, I don't know what it was. Like he was seeing something only a dying man could see."

Bradley flicked cigar ash into the sink. "The shooter was over by the window, is that right?"

Franklin stared up at him, perplexed. "How did you know that?"

"The bullet holes. I assumed you were shooting at someone."

"That's right, I was."

"Any luck?"

"What d'you mean?"

"You score any hits, George?"

"No, I don't think so. I don't think I even came close to hitting the guy."

"It was a man?" Bradley had spoken more sharply than he'd intended, but Franklin hadn't seemed to notice.

"Yeah, it was a man."

"What'd he look like, George?"

"I remember exactly what he looked like."

"That's good," said Bradley. "Do you think you could describe him for us?"

"He was wearing a shoulder-length wig."

Bradley nodded, waiting. Franklin crossed his legs and leaned back against the tank of the toilet.

Finally Willows said, "What colour was the wig?"

"Silvery blonde."

"Platinum?" said Bradley.

"Yeah, platinum. A wig. Shiny, artificial. Like that stuff they put on Christmas trees, almost."

"Okay," said Bradley. "We're doing pretty good so far. What else can you give us?"

"What else do you want to know?"

"Well, what was he wearing?"

"You mean, other than the wig?"

"Yes."

"He had a mauve raincoat made out of some kind of plastic material, and a pair of gloves."

"What kind of gloves?"

"White ones."

"Leather?"

"I don't remember. His shoes were leather, though. White leather, with high heels. Spikes."

"He was wearing women's shoes?"

"Of course."

"But you're sure it was a man."

Franklin nodded.

"A man in drag," said Bradley.

"You got it, Inspector."

"Now that we know what he was wearing, George, why don't we see if we can remember what he looked like."

"Good idea," said Franklin.

Bradley darted Willows a quick, indecipherable look, and then said, "Was he wearing any makeup?"

"A lot," said Franklin.

"How tall would you say he was?"

"Hard to say." Franklin took the cigarette out of his mouth. Ash tumbled down his chest and across his stomach. He brushed at it ineffectually.

"Take a guess," prompted Bradley.

"The guy was half out of the window when I came into the room. He could've been a midget for all I know. All I saw was his clothes and his face under the hat."

"What hat?" said Bradley.

"Didn't I tell you he was wearing a hat?"

"No, I don't think so."

Franklin looked at Willows, seeking confirmation.

"Tell us about the hat," said Willows.

"Sure," said Franklin.

Bradley chewed on his cigar. He spat a fleck of tobacco into the sink. "We're all ears, George."

"It was white, a floppy white hat with a wide brim. Like a woman might wear out in the garden, in the summer."

"Must've been hard to see his face, under a hat like that."

"Yeah, I guess so."

"But you're sure it was a man, that it was a man wearing makeup and a woman's clothes."

"See, he probably heard me coming down the hall. He was looking right at me when I came into the room, as if he was expecting me. And that's when I saw his face, the face of a clown."

"How d'you mean, George?"

"He had big pink spots on his cheeks, and he was wearing too much lipstick. When he smiled at me, his mouth seemed to stretch right across his face. There was lipstick on his teeth, they were stained red with it. At first I thought it was Dave's blood, that he'd been feeding on Dave." Franklin paused to light a fresh cigarette from the stump of the old. "Can I go get an ashtray?" he said to Willows.

"Use the sink," said Bradley. "You said he smiled at you?"

"Right."

"Then what?"

"The duck started quacking again. A terrible noise, wet, choking. I stood there listening to it, and I couldn't understand how a child's toy could make a noise like that. I thought I must be going crazy. And then I saw that the man in the window had a rifle, and that he was pointing it at me. . . ."

"Keep going, George."

"We looked at each other. The duck screamed. And then that fucking gun went off, and I felt the heat of the muzzle blast and I knew that I was dead."

Hunched on the toilet seat, Franklin stared once more into the barrel of the rifle. His face was slick with sweat, lumpy, bloated with remorse, colourless except for a faint subterranean tinge of glaucous blue. He gave Willows an odd, accusing look. "How could he have missed me, Jack?"

"Better him than us," said Willows. The bathroom was thick with smoke. He opened the door a few inches and looked out. The hallway was empty. He opened the door a little wider.

"You leaving?" said Franklin anxiously.

"Not until you do."

"After he shot at me, he turned his back on me and climbed the

81

rest of the way out the window and crouched on the ledge. I could see he was going to jump. He spread his arms. I took a bead on that big white hat he was wearing, and pulled the trigger. The gun went off but he didn't move. I aimed at the middle of his back and fired at him and fired again and kept firing until my gun was empty. Then I saw that he was gone."

"Then what, you went over to the window?"

"No, I couldn't."

"Why not, George?"

"Because it wasn't the duck I heard making that wet noise. And it wasn't the duck that was screaming, either. It was my partner, it was Dave."

Bradley took the cigar out of his mouth and massaged his face. "Just one more question, George."

"Shoot," said Franklin.

"When Dave was inside the walk-in closet, did he turn on the light?"

"What light?" said Franklin.

"Never mind," said Bradley. "Forget it." He'd taken a quick look in the closet while Milne was working on Atkinson's corpse. There was a ceiling fixture, but when he'd flicked the switch the light had not come on. Tapping the bulb gently with the tip of his ballpoint pen, he'd discovered it was loose, that it was only screwed partway into the socket. The closet had been deep, the racks jammed with clothes. It would have been easy for the killer to hide there, easy for Atkinson to miss him.

The Closet Killer. Wonderful. He could already see the headlines. Sighing inwardly, Bradley stood up. He rubbed the small of his back, massaging away the stiffness. "Tell Goldstein to check the closet for prints," he said to Willows. "Make sure he dusts down the light bulb and the wall in the area of the electric switchplate."

"Okay," said Willows.

Bradley looked down at Franklin. Franklin was sitting on the lid of the toilet with the posture of a man who was prepared to sit for ever. Bradley indicated Franklin and said, "You better take him downtown. Get a statement from him and then take him home."

Willows tapped Franklin on the shoulder. "Let's go, George."

Franklin nodded wearily. Willows helped him to his feet, and at the same time reached deftly under his raincoat and took away his gun.

Franklin gave him a surprised and wounded look.

"Regulations," said Willows. "Nothing personal."

"I want it back as soon as possible," said Franklin. "I'm gonna need it to get the guy who shot Dave."

"Don't worry about that," said Willows. "We'll get him."

"Blow his head off," said Franklin. He thumped a fist into his open hand, and then sat wearily back down on the toilet.

Atkinson's body lay on the stretcher in a dark green plastic bodybag. One of the ambulance guys smiled at Parker as he yanked on the bag's zipper. "Teeth must be out of alignment," he said, and gave her a wink.

Appreciative chuckles from his partner. A wide grin from Farley Spears. A snigger from the cop lounging in the doorway. Even a little twitch of the lip from Jerry Goldstein. Parker didn't get the joke until they wheeled the stretcher around and she saw Atkinson's upper plate leering at her.

In the bathroom, Mel Dutton was using the Nikon with the 28mm lens to take a series of photographs of the dead goldfish floating in the toilet bowl. He was conducting a little experiment, bouncing his flash off the bathroom wall in order to cast the far side of the bowl in deep shadow. Each time he took a picture, the top of his bald skull glowed with an incandescent brilliance, as if lit from within by a sturdy filament of bones.

IX

WOHLFORD SWUNG FLUIDLY, from the hips. The ball seemed to jump off the end of his bat. Freddy could tell by the sound of the blow that it was on its way to the upper decks. Outta there. They all sounded the same, homers. You heard one, you'd heard 'em all.

Freddy turned his back on the television as Wohlford rounded third base. Wohlford was smiling, and Freddy was smiling too. He had twenty bucks on the game and it was six-zip Toronto, bottom of the eighth.

Freddy reached out and hooked a bottle of Cutty Sark towards him with his left hand, a hand that was slick with scar tissue. A lot of people stared at the hand, and Freddy didn't blame them. The hand was mangled real bad, the three middle fingers chewed off right down to the knuckles — the stumps so short he had to wear his wedding ring on his thumb. Freddy took two glasses from the mirrored shelf behind him and poured an ounce of Cutty free-hand into each glass, then deliberately splashed in another half-measure. Freddy picked up the two glasses, balancing them in the palm of his good hand, and started towards Jack Willows, who was sitting as always in the end booth with his back to the wall.

Freddy was still twenty feet away when Willows saw him moving in, and whatever it was that Willows was saying to the woman sitting opposite him, he let it drop. Freddy was curious, and he guessed it showed. Willows drank a fair amount but since Norm Burroughs had dropped out of the picture, Willows had been drinking alone. Until now, that is. Freddy checked out the woman as he placed the drinks on the table.

"Thanks, Freddy," said Willows, dismissing him.

"You folks ready for something to eat?" said Freddy. He smiled at the woman. She'd noticed his hand but she wasn't

84

staring at it or away from it, and he liked that. "Maybe something to nibble on, a bowl of peanuts?"

"Nothing," said Willows.

"Call me if you change your mind," said Freddy, still looking at the woman. He gave the table a quick wipe with the damp cloth he carried slung over his arm, and then turned away, heading back to the bar. He'd catch the last of the baseball and then maybe go back with a plate of chicken wings hot out of the microwave. See if Willows would swap a free meal for an introduction to his new friend. Freddy had heard a rumour that Willows was having serious problems with his marriage. Maybe she was the reason why.

Parker waited until Freddy had moved out of earshot and then nudged the twenty-dollar bill that Willows had dropped on the table when they'd first sat down, and that had remained untouched through three rounds. "I'm kind of surprised they let you run up a tab in a place like this," she said.

Willows tilted his glass. He watched the glass fall away from the Scotch, the ice settle. After a moment he let the glass swing back to a vertical position. He put the glass down on the table. "Freddy and I go back a long way," he said at last.

Parker waited. Now that she'd got him talking, she wasn't going to rush him.

Willows sipped at his drink and then said, "Freddy used to make a pretty heavy dollar working the piano bars around town. But he was one of those guys, when he wasn't working, he liked to play. And he didn't much care who he was playing with, if you know what I mean."

"He got mixed up with the wrong crowd?"

"The wrong woman," said Willows. "You know the Redstone Hotel, over on Cordova?"

Parker nodded. The Redstone rented rooms by the day or by the hour. It was a dump.

"About two years ago, the night clerk dialled a 911, told the dispatcher he had a customer sounded like he was in more than the usual amount of pain. Norm and I caught the squeal, drove down there." Willows shook his head, remembering. "That was the only night clerk I ever met who had a talent for understatement."

85

Parker smiled. "How d'you mean?"

"Freddy had checked into a room on the third floor, right at the back of the building. But we could hear him down in the lobby just as clearly as if he was standing next to us. He was screaming his head off. He sounded as if he was dying. You ever been in the Redstone?"

"Not yet," said Parker.

"It's the kind of place, even if there was an elevator, it wouldn't work. Norm and I pulled our guns and ran up three flights of stairs, down the hall. The door was locked. Norm kicked it in, and in we went." Willows drained his glass. "Freddy was sitting on the floor by the window, chained to the radiator. There were three other guys in the room, and a woman. The woman and one of the men were lying on the bed, drinking from a bottle of Red Devil wine. The other two guys were kneeling on either side of Freddy. One of them was holding him down while his buddy was feeding what was left of Freddy's hand into an electric blender."

Parker glanced behind her, at Freddy working the bar, happily mixing drinks. "Why were they hurting him, what had he done?"

"Screwed around with the wrong guy's wife." Willows smiled. "He said at the trial he'd never understand why they stuck his fingers into that machine, instead of a more relevant appendage."

Parker laughed, perhaps a shade too loudly. She became alarmed. Was it possible she'd already had one too many? She looked down at her glass and saw that it was almost empty. So far, she'd had no more than two or possibly three drinks. Four at the most. She wondered if Willows might be trying to get her drunk. Somehow it didn't seem his style. She finished her drink and put the empty glass down on the table, pushing it away from her, watching it glide smoothly across the varnished wood on interlocking rings of condensation. Looking up, she found Willows staring at her.

"Something on your mind?" she said.

Willows nodded. He looked serious.

"What is it?"

"Yesterday morning," said Willows, "I ran into Shelley Rice in the service elevator at 312 Main. Or maybe I should say that Rice ran into me. He was on his way to a holding cell. He'd been busted.

86

Possession with intent. You happen to know a couple of narcotics cops named Orwell and Kearns?"

"I know them."

"You turn them on to Rice?"

"Yes."

"Why?"

"Why not?" said Parker.

Willows stared hard at her for a moment and then slid out of the booth. He walked a few steps away from her and then changed his mind and came back and sat down beside her. His hip pressed up against hers, but there was no warmth in his eyes. She moved a little closer to the wall, putting a bit of space between them, and at the same time turned to face him more squarely. He picked up her empty glass and made the ice rattle, then put the glass back down. "Look, when we were at Rice's house, I told him that if he cooperated with us we wouldn't give him any trouble. I gave him my word that we weren't interested in drugs, and you heard me do it."

"You gave him your word," said Parker. "I didn't give him mine."

"That's bullshit. We're supposed to be partners. I was speaking for both of us."

"No you weren't. You might've thought you were, but you were wrong. For Christ's sake, Rice was a dealer!"

"That isn't the point."

"It damn well is," said Parker angrily. "It's exactly the point."

They were sitting so close together that Willows could see tiny flecks of gold in Parker's eyes. He thought for a moment and then said, "What if Rice hadn't been a dealer, what if he'd been a pimp. Would you have handed him over to vice?"

"No," said Parker firmly.

"So you weren't just out to score some points. There's more to it than that. You've got something against dealers. Something personal?"

"A brother who's a junkie," said Parker. She gave that a moment to sink in and then said, "Now you tell me something. Does the fact that Norm Burroughs was buried this afternoon

87

have anything at all to do with the hard time you've been giving me?"

Willows stared at her, stunned into silence. Finally he said, "How did you know about Norm?"

"I was there," said Parker.

"Why?"

"He was your old partner. I'm your new partner. It seemed like the right thing to do, that's all."

"He told me you visited him in the ward."

"Just once. We didn't get along too well."

"Norm was like that," said Willows. "He was a spiky bastard, didn't have a lot of friends."

Willows smiled, and Parker said, "What are you grinning about, what's so funny?"

Willows hesitated, and then started to tell her about the night he and Burroughs had deliberately rammed a moving freight train, destroying a brand-new squad car with less than fifty miles on the odometer.

Behind the bar, Freddy was using his remote to flip through the channels when a flurry of motion caught his eye. It was Willows' date, waving a couple of empty glasses in the air, signalling for fresh drinks. Freddy put the remote down on the counter. He waved back, scar tissue shiny under the lights, then popped the chicken in the micro and reached for the bottle of Cutty Sark.

X

ANDY PATTERSON'S FRIDAY shift started at four in the afternoon and ended at two in the morning. By ten o'clock that night he'd run less than a hundred dollars through the meter. Worse, he'd spent most of his free time cruising restlessly around the city. Boredom had kept his foot on the gas pedal. It had also pushed his mileage total far beyond the acceptable limit. If he hoped to avoid catching an earful from the cab's owner, he was going to have to spend the rest of the night roosting, not move an inch.

Turning left off Hemlock, Patterson drove west down Broadway to Granville and parked in the two-cab stand in front of the Royal Bank. The rain continued to belt ferociously down. Traffic was light, the sidewalks deserted. He radioed the dispatcher and told him he'd be out of service for a few minutes, and then turned off the engine. Using the business section of the evening newspaper to keep his head dry, he got out of the cab and ran around the corner to the VIP newstand.

When he came in through the door, the elderly Hungarian woman at the cash register smiled at him and reached behind her for the two packs of menthol cigarettes he bought every night he worked. Patterson paid her out of his tip money, exchanged a few words about the weather, and hurried back to his cab. Smoking, he waited for a break in the radio traffic and then cleared himself with the dispatcher.

Across the street, an old lady carrying an armful of bright yellow daffodils came out of the Aristocratic restaurant. She didn't have an umbrella and she wasn't wearing a hat, but she paid no attention to the rain. A native, thought Patterson. He watched her walk slowly down Broadway and then disappear into the lane behind the restaurant. Settling back into his seat, he opened the paper to the sports section. James Lawton's column

89

was on golf, a game Patterson had never played and had no interest in playing. He flicked cigarette ash to the floor of the car and began to read.

Twenty minutes later, his call number came over the radio. Dropping the paper on the seat, Patterson picked up the mike and acknowledged the call. The dispatcher directed him to the Penthouse, a downtown cabaret. The club was a little more than a mile away, but it was a straight run over the Granville Street bridge and down the Seymour off-ramp. He'd be there in two minutes, three at the most.

Judith and Sidney were standing in the scant shelter of the big, old-fashioned Penthouse sign when Patterson swung his cab sharply into the curb lane in front of the club. The sign had flashing red arrows above the name of the club, which was written in green neon. More red neon advertised the continuing presence of GIRLS GIRLS GIRLS. The main attraction of the evening was,

NANCY BON BON

RARE & BARE

Sid hurriedly stepped forward as the cab pulled up to the curb. The gaudy neon of the club's Eagletime clock stained his face blue and yellow, his teeth pink. Turning up the collar of his trenchcoat, he pulled Judith across the sidewalk, through the rain. Behind them, an emaciated pimp in a popsicle-coloured suit burst through the club's double doors on the dead run. There was a wide gap between his front teeth. He used it to whistle shrilly. His bug eyes were fixed on the taxi. Sid was in a race, and he knew it. Yanking the back door of the cab open, he pushed Judith inside and fell in after her, slammed the door shut and locked it. Out on the sidewalk, the pimp screamed abuse and jumped up and down in his alligator shoes. Sid smiled, and blew him a kiss. The pimp reached under his coat. Patterson dropped the meter and put his foot down on the gas. The cab shot away from the curb. Patterson glanced in his rearview mirror. "Where to, folks?"

Sid looked at Judith. "Your place or mine?" he said.

"Whatever's closest."

Sid grinned. "You think you can find eleven-twenty Jervis, cabbie?"

Patterson nodded. The light at Smithe was red. He braked, noted the time and address of the fare on his call sheet, spoke softly into his mike. The dispatcher responded immediately. The light changed to green and Patterson turned left on to Smithe. In the back seat, Sid laughed and Judith giggled. Patterson heard the faint rustle of clothing, and took another quick look in the mirror. He guessed Sid's age at about thirty-five. Sid's hair was beginning to thin, and he was a few pounds overweight. But he wasn't a bad-looking guy, in a meaty kind of way. Patterson noticed that Sid had removed his trenchcoat and that it now lay across his lap. Sid's right arm was across Judith's shoulder, his hand rested on the back of her neck. Patterson saw the soft, lightly tanned skin above her collarbone dimple briefly as Sid's fingers played a nervous tune on her flesh.

Patterson slowed to let a black El Camino ease into his lane. He shifted slightly in his seat, and his Van Halen T-shirt made a faint rippling noise as it came unglued from the vinyl. The interior of the cab was like a sauna. He turned off the heater and rolled the window down a few inches, took another quick peek in the mirror. Judith had a mop of thick blonde hair that was cut short in a way that emphasized the narrowness of her face, giving her a waifish look. Her eyes were cornflower blue. She had a wide, pouty mouth. She might be nineteen, but Patterson doubted if she was twenty.

Ahead of him, the Camino signalled a left turn and slowed for the oncoming traffic. The light turned yellow. The Camino accelerated down Comox past the hospital, leaving them at the intersection, caught by the red.

Patterson slowly became aware that Judith was watching him. Their eyes met in the mirror. Before he could look away, she wet her lips with the tip of her tongue and gave him a small, secret smile.

Behind them, a car honked angrily. Patterson looked up, and saw that the light had turned to green. He hit the gas, accelerated through the intersection. In the back seat, Judith laughed softly.

Five minutes later, the taxi pulled into the wide, semi-circular driveway in front of Sid's apartment block. The huge lobby, encased in towering sheets of plate glass which rose from ground level all the way to the thirty-foot high ceiling, was brightly illuminated by a massive chandelier. Light splashed through the immense windows, across the sidewalk and into the cab. Andy Patterson stopped half a car-length behind a bone-white Corvette convertible. The car was empty and its hazard lights were flashing.

Patterson turned off the meter and put the gearshift lever in park. Twisting in his seat, he caught a glimpse of a large brown nipple as Judith unhurriedly buttoned her blouse. Sid, his face empty and smirking, fumbled with his wallet. He pulled out a crisp new ten-dollar bill, crumpled it in his fist and tossed it negligently at Patterson.

"Keep the change, pal."

Patterson looked down at the money lying on the seat beside him. He didn't say anything. He reached for his pack of cigarettes, lit up.

On the far side of the street, fifty feet away, a rusty maroon-coloured Ford LTD pulled up to the curb. The driver rolled down his window. His blonde wig reflected light from the distant chandelier as he turned to look at the cab. Picking up the Winchester, he slid a cartridge into the breech and pushed home the bolt. A few drops of machine oil had leaked from his rifle to the upholstery of the seat. He rubbed the oil with the ball of his thumb, smearing it, driving it deeply into the fabric.

Sid opened the rear door of the cab.

The sniper rested his forearm on the Ford's door sill, peered into the telescopic sight.

Sid stepped out of the cab and into the crosshairs of the scope. He was fumbling with his trenchcoat, shaking out the folds so he could throw the coat over his shoulders to protect himself from the rain.

Judith, as she followed Sid out of the cab, trailed her hand through Patterson's hair, across the nape of his neck. In the same moment, she gave him a look that made it clear she'd much rather be spending her time with him.

Patterson was amazed. He was short, pudgy, shaped like a pear. It was obvious that he was gay. Why would she be interested in him? Why would she even bother to pretend to be interested in him?

The rear door of the cab was wide open. Sid hadn't bothered to shut it. Patterson watched as Judith leaned against the glass door of the lobby. He saw the wash of relief on Sid's face as Sid found his keys. Through the windscreen, Patterson saw Sid push open the door, saw Sid and Judith hurry hand in hand into the brightly lit glass bowl of the lobby, across the polished marble floor towards the bank of elevators.

Patterson unfastened his seatbelt and reached behind him, straining as he groped for the handle of the open door. Grunting, he stretched an extra inch backwards. His fingertips touched cold metal.

The first bullet punched a neat hole in the side window and then disintegrated as it sheared through the vertical steel support post on the far side of the car. Fragments of metal ricocheted off the sidewalk.

The sniper fired again.

The window split into a thousand precariously balanced pieces and then collapsed. The air hummed and vibrated. The left side of Patterson's face went numb. He brought his hand to his cheek. His fingers slid across warm, wet flesh. He realized that he had been shot, and reacted instinctively, without conscious thought.

His hands slapped wildly at the steering wheel and gearshift lever, his foot jabbed hard at the gas pedal. The taxi lurched forward, striking the Corvette at an angle and tearing away half the rear deck. Chunks of fibreglass and plastic rained down on the cab's yellow hood. The Corvette's surviving tail-light flashed at an accelerated rate.

Panicked, Patterson kept his foot on the gas pedal and never thought of putting the transmission in reverse. The taxi bulled the Corvette slowly forward, then slipped away and veered sharply towards the lobby. Patterson heard a shot. He felt the cab lurch as the left rear tyre blew out. A shower of bright orange sparks bounced across the sidewalk. A hubcap whirled straight up into the night, shrieking madly. Patterson fought the wheel as the taxi burst through the huge plate-glass windows in an explosion of glass, skidded sideways across the marble floor and shuddered to a stop directly beneath the enormous chandelier. His elbow hit the meter and knocked down the flag. The big red numbers blossomed on the display screen, began to turn over dime by dime.

There was a moment of silence, and then another thirty-foot panel of glass collapsed in a welter of shards and splinters that dropped hissing and spinning to shatter on the marble. Patterson lay across the seat, his right arm tucked awkwardly beneath him at an impossible angle.

The sniper, peering through the rain and into the haze of light, caught a flicker of movement inside the cab. A bloody hand rose slowly into view, clawed at the rearview mirror. The sniper fired, and the mirror vanished in a red and silver froth. He opened the door of the Ford and stepped into the street. A gust of wind tugged at the broad brim of his hat, ruffled the lace trim of the white dress.

Standing in the middle of the road, pelted by the rain and buffeted by the wind, he fired steadily into the body of the cab. Spent brass tinkled on the asphalt as he emptied one magazine after another. When he had fired a dozen rounds, he paused to scrutinize the taxi through the Lyman scope. The front door on the driver's side was shot to pieces. The big, soft-nose bullets had fragmented on impact with the sheet metal and ripped through the interior of the cab with all the force of a shotgun blast.

Balancing on one foot, the sniper kicked out. His right shoe described a shallow arc and landed in the gutter on the far side of the street. He turned and climbed back into the Ford, slammed shut the door. He released the emergency brake, depressed the clutch pedal, put the car in gear and revved the eight-cylinder motor. The valves clattered noisily. The exhaust vented a cloud of greasy blue smoke. He eased out the clutch. As the Ford started down the street, the rain suddenly doubled in volume, cobbling the windscreen and lashing down at him through the open window.

The car slowly picked up speed. The sniper was just about to shift into second gear when something small and furry bolted into the glare of the headlights. He hit the brakes and then accelerated as the creature, a racoon the size of a large cat, stared at him with luminous green eyes from the safety of the boulevard.

From the moment the first shot was fired, Sid and Judith had stood transfixed against the far wall of the lobby, next to the bank of elevators. As the sniper kicked free of the high-heeled shoe and turned to get back into the Ford, Judith broke free of Sid's grasp. He cried out as she ran lightly across the field of glass and outside, into the middle of the circular driveway.

The Ford, trailing a stratus of burnt oil, continued steadily down Jervis.

Judith, searching frantically through her purse, came at last upon her platinum Sheaffer, a fat booklet of personalized cheques. Rain plastered her golden hair to her scalp and trickled down into her eyes as she squinted into the night. The licence number was, she thought, GHN 121. She uncapped the pen. The Ford's brake lights flared an angry red. For a terrifying fraction of a second, Judith thought the sniper had seen her in his rearview mirror. Then she saw that an animal had run in front of the car and that the driver had braked to avoid hitting it. Trembling, she scribbled the plate number down on the back of the chequebook.

"Judith!"

Turning, she saw Sid standing on the sidewalk where it was bisected by the curving driveway. He shouted her name again, and wildly waved his arms. She saw that the rain and fitful wind had played havoc with his artfully arranged hair. He was very thin on top, almost bald. He took an uncertain step towards her. Suddenly he was bathed in light. Judith heard a sound behind her, the roar of an engine. She spun on her heel, stumbled, and sat down in the middle of the road. The lights were aimed straight at her now, blinding her, pinning her to the asphalt. She stared, horrified, as the police car raced towards her, fishtailing crazily from side to side, dome and headlights flashing out of sync with the piercing scream of the siren.

Judith scrambled to her feet. She twisted an ankle and sat down again.

The onrushing car swerved sharply away from her at the last possible second. Judith heard the shrill whine of tyres on pavement. She was splattered with rainwater. The nearside bumper missed her by fractions of an inch, the chrome flashing incredibly bright.

Sid's face went slack with fear as the squad car abruptly skewed towards him. He tried to run, but found to his horror that he had forgotten how to bend his knees. He opened his mouth.

He screamed, and heard nothing but the scream of the siren.

XI

BECAUSE IT WAS standard departmental policy to team the young with the old and so temper foolhardiness with caution, Paul Furth and Chris Lambert should not have been riding together the night that Andy Patterson was shot and killed.

Furth and Lambert were both rookies, with less than six months' seniority between them. But Furth's regular partner had come down with the flu less than an hour into their shift, and since the police union insisted on two men to a car during the night hours, the sick man had to be replaced. And that's why Lambert had found himself temporarily reassigned from his usual shift as a foot patrolman on the south end of the Granville Street mall. So far, he hadn't missed the dime baggers, amateur musicians, feisty drunks or bulk-rate hookers one little bit.

As Furth drove slowly around the block-square perimeter of Nelson Park, Lambert thought about how nice it felt to have a roof over his head and a cushion under his ass, a steady flow of warm air across his feet. He glanced at Furth, envying him the luck of his assignment. They turned south on Thurlow. Over on Jervis, the shooting started.

Furth gunned the engine, turned right on Comox and stopped halfway up the block, at a distance from the noisy flow of traffic on Thurlow. Pulling the squad car over to the curb, he turned off the engine and rolled down his window.

The second shot came almost immediately. Lambert opened his mouth to ask Furth why they were just sitting there not doing anything, but before he could speak there was the sound of a collision — the taxi pummelling the white Corvette.

Furth started the engine of the squad car.

Close behind the sound of the third shot came the crash of the taxi hurtling through the floor-to-ceiling windows, an avalanche of shattered glass.

"What the hell was that!" said Lambert.

"Shut up!" snapped Furth, his head cocked to one side, listening.

Another string of shots bounced and echoed off the surrounding highrises. The acoustics were too tricky to get an exact fix on the location, but Furth guessed that the shooter was less than two blocks away, probably on either Jervis or Broughton. He hit all the switches and put the gas pedal to the floor. The Dodge Aspen leapt forward, lights blazing through the rain, siren wailing at a fever pitch.

Lambert shifted his weight to his left hip, and drew his revolver. He felt very, very good. And why not? So far, all he had to his credit was a mixed bag of jaywalkers and drunks. Hardly the stuff of rapid promotions and a meteoric climb through the ranks. But now, for the first time in his short and unremarkable career, he was involved in some meaningful police work. He flipped open the cylinder of his revolver and checked the load. Furth glanced at him, but didn't say anything.

There were several more shots, each one a little louder than the last. Furth counted three, then a short pause and then three more.

"Left on Jervis!" said Lambert.

Furth was already spinning the wheel. The rear tyres skidded on the wet pavement. He overcorrected and the car slewed sideways, rocking on its springs. The street was narrow, crammed on both sides with parked cars. The steering wheel twitched under Furth's hands as the squad car's rear bumper grazed the flank of a carelessly parked station wagon. Furth heard metal grind against metal. He swore loudly, but kept his foot down on the gas.

Furth had just managed to bring the Aspen under control when he saw Judith sitting cross-legged in the middle of the road, spotlighted in the rapidly narrowing beam of his lights. He yanked at the wheel and the Aspen drifted sideways, tyres slithering. Furth caught a brief glimpse of a strained white face, big blue eyes. Then they were screaming down the sidewalk in hot pursuit of a maroon Ford, the wheels on Furth's side tearing through the uncut spring grass and bumping over the roots of the big chestnut trees that lined the boulevard. An indistinct grey shape ran along a branch a few feet above them, stopped and seemed to double in size. Furth had a fleeting impression of emerald eyes and a toothpaste snarl.

"What the fuck was that?"

"You know something?" said Lambert. "You're really weird."

"What d'you mean?"

"That guy back there on the sidewalk, you missed him by inches and didn't even blink. Then you see a racoon sitting in a tree and go crazy."

"Wait a minute," said Furth. "What guy on the sidewalk?"

"The bald guy," said Lambert.

Furth didn't know anything about Lambert, he had no way of telling if he was kidding him or what. He decided not to worry about the bald man until later, when he wasn't so busy driving. Down at the far end of the block, the Ford was making a left turn. Just for a moment, Furth wondered why the car had managed to gain so little ground on them. Then he had the Dodge burning rubber, engine howling as the car shuddered through a tight ninety-degree turn and hurtled down the slippery, blackly-gleaming street.

Lambert, eyes bright, was hunched on the edge of his seat, his revolver clenched in his hand.

Furth leaned over and punched him hard on the shoulder. "Get on the radio, let's get some backup down here!"

"Calm down," said Lambert, sounding annoyed. He reached for the microphone, picked it up and pressed the transmit button, then sighed and lowered the mike.

"Something wrong?" said Furth.

Lambert gave him a lopsided grin. "I got no idea where we are. How can I call for backup when I don't know where to send them?"

"Shit," said Furth. He pumped the brakes and then hit the gas again. They rocketed down the straight, closing fast on the maroon Ford. "We're heading south on Bute," he shouted at Lambert, "between Pendrell and Davie!"

"Pendrell and what?"

"South on Bute!" screamed Furth. "South on Bute!"

They caught the light on Davie, crossing on the green seconds after the Ford had raced through the red, and then Furth saw the flare of brake lights as the Ford swung left on Burnaby. They roared past a parked squad car, but there was no one inside. The Ford turned down Thurlow. A block away, Pacific led straight to Burrard Bridge and the maze of Kitsilano.

"Get a roadblock set up on the other side of the bridge!" yelled Furth.

"What bridge?"

"The Burrard Street bridge!"

"Okay," said Lambert, "take it easy." He lifted the mike to his lips and pressed the transmit button, at the same time using his gun hand to brace himself against the dashboard. Fifty feet in front of them, a woman wearing a bright yellow rain slicker bicycled out of an alley and into their path. They were travelling south, down the steep slope that led to the mouth of False Creek. The Dodge aquaplaned down the hill on overlapping sheets of rainwater, fighting gravity and a lack of traction. A collision seemed inevitable.

In his mind's eye, Lambert saw the car hit the bike, saw the girl cartwheel gracefully over the handlebars and under the onrushing wheels of the police car. He wondered what she could possibly have been thinking of, not to have heard the siren or seen the lights.

At the last possible second the girl took evasive action, twisting her front wheel sharply to the left. A thin layer of gravel had been washed out of the mouth of the alley by the continuing rain. The bike skidded, wobbled, and went over on its side. The girl hit the asphalt and rolled. Furth took a right at Harwood, and accelerated. The Dodge surged forward. Lambert twisted in his seat to look behind him, but the girl was already lost from view.

Furth wasn't exactly sure why, but they had continued to gain on the Ford. It was less than two hundred yards in front of them when the driver suddenly cut his lights and turned right up an alley. Furth braked hard, and swung in behind him.

The alley was typical of the West End — narrow, filled with potholes, crowded on both sides with illegally parked cars. The Ford reached the far end of the block and raced through the intersection, a dark, fleeting shadow. Furth charged after it, his foot on the gas and his heart in his mouth.

Without warning, the Ford suddenly turned sharply right and vanished. Furth felt his stomach muscles tighten. Chasing the bastard had been bad enough, but now they had come to the gristly part, catching him. He hit the brakes and the Aspen lurched to a stop at the lip of a steeply-pitched driveway that led down to the underground garage of a newish three-storey condominium. The Ford was at the bottom of the driveway, parked at an angle with its front bumper up against the garage's steel mesh security door.

"Now we've got him," exulted Lambert.

Furth wouldn't have bet money on it. There were floodlights mounted in the concrete retaining walls on either side of the garage entrance, and more lights scattered among the ornamental shrubbery at the top of the walls, but none of the lights were working. The Ford was hidden in deep shadow, and somehow Furth doubted this was a lucky accident. He flicked a switch, and the quartz spotlight mounted on the right front fender blazed into life. He started to crank the beam around to focus on the Ford. A hot orange gout of flame spouted from somewhere near the front of the Ford. The spotlight disintegrated in an explosion of glass and metal fragments. Shrapnel starred the Apsen's windscreen.

Lambert yanked open his door. The inside light came on. He bailed out into the rain, Furth right behind him. The sound of the rifle shot echoed down the alley. Furth kicked the door shut, and the inside light went out. He drew his revolver. His hands were shaking.

"What about the shotgun?" said Lambert.

"It's in the boot."

"Well, go get it."

"You get it, if you need it so bad."

"Where's the key?"

"The key's in the ignition. You want it, all you have to do is climb back inside the car. But you can't do that without opening the door. And when you open the door, the inside light's gonna come on. You see what I'm getting at, Lambert?"

"You're saying we can probably get along without the shotgun."

"Exactly," said Furth. He hefted his revolver. He was pleased to see that his hands had steadied. "We got the guy trapped. All we have to do is keep him pinned down until the reinforcements get here, right?"

"I guess so," said Lambert doubtfully.

"We got a problem I don't know about?"

"Not really," said Lambert. He gave Furth a twisted, watered-down grin. "It's just that after you almost hit that girl on the bike, things got a little mixed up."

"What're you getting at?"

"Well . . ."

"You didn't call in, did you?"

"To tell the truth," said Lambert, "I'm not too sure one way or the other. Do you remember me not calling in?"

"No," said Furth, "I don't."

"Well then, maybe I did."

"Wonderful," said Furth. "What that means is maybe some-body's on the way and maybe they aren't." He heard the faint drone of an electric motor, a low-pitched hum.

"What's that noise?" said Lambert.

"The garage door," said Furth. Turning his back on Lambert, he hurried towards the rear of the squad car in a graceless, waddling crouch.

Lambert knelt down and peered under the belly of the Aspen, but was unable to see down to the bottom of the driveway. There was a sudden explosion off to his right. Startled, he banged his head against the underside of the car frame. His hat fell off, into an oily puddle. He picked the hat up and put it back on at a rakish angle. There was another shot. Furth was firing blindly over the boot of the squad car at the Ford.

Lambert scuttled around to the front of the squad car. He took a quick look down the driveway, orienting himself, and then began to shoot, pulling the trigger of his .38 so quickly that the

102

individual explosions seemed to merge together, bouncing off the surrounding buildings in a long, continuous roar. When his gun was empty he risked another quick peek over the hood of the Aspen.

"See anything?" whispered Furth.

"The garage door's stopped moving."

"How high off the ground is it?"

"A foot, maybe a foot and a half."

"You see any movement down there?"

"Nope," said Lambert. He ejected his spent shells and reloaded.

"You think we got him?"

"How the hell should I know? You want to take a hike down there and check it out?"

Furth pretended to think about it, taking his time. He became aware that they had gathered an audience, that they were being watched. He looked up and saw that dozens of people were watching them from the windows and balconies of the surrounding apartment blocks and condominiums. He waved at an elderly couple on the far side of the alley. The man shifted his grip on his cane, and waved back. Furth took a bead on the near front tyre of the Ford and let off two rounds. The tyre burst as he fired his second shot, the rush of escaping air sounding like a final, dying breath.

Furth kept shooting until his revolver was empty and he was out of ammunition. "Cover me," he said to Lambert, and holstered his weapon and stood up. It seemed faintly ridiculous to continue hiding behind the Aspen while all around him people stood exposed and unafraid. Lambert stood too. Furth watched him shoot, listened to the heavy thud of the bullets hitting the Ford. Another tyre blew out, and the vehicle lurched as if it had been mortally wounded. Furth trotted around to the driver's door of the Aspen. He yanked the door open, grabbed the keys out of the ignition and hustled back to the rear of the car to open the boot.

Lambert shot out the Ford's windshield. There was scattered applause from the crowd.

Furth got the boot open and hauled out the shotgun, a pump-action Browning. As he loaded the gun, he heard the infant scream of a dozen approaching sirens, and knew that he and Lambert were running out of time. He worked the slide action of the Browning, swung the barrel around to bear on the Ford, and fired from the hip. The steel mesh security door rattled under the impact of the shot. Furth heard glass breaking somewhere deep inside the garage. He adjusted his elevation considerably and let off another round. The load of buckshot struck festive sparks and streamers of light off the ramp and the concrete floor of the garage. At a range of approximately fifteen yards, Furth had managed to miss twice in a row.

Someone on one of the balconies, a bearded man in underpants standing out there in the rain, shouted words that were unintelligible but clearly not flattering.

Furth pressed the butt-plate of the Browning firmly against his shoulder. Nestling his cheek against the stock, he aimed carefully and then fired four times in quick succession, as fast as he could work the slide.

There was a deafening explosion, and the Ford was suddenly enveloped in a huge, rising ball of flame.

Furth staggered backwards, raising his hands to protect his face from the scorching heat. The cedar wall of the condo above the garage began to smoke. A secondary explosion blew the hood off the Ford. The ornamental shrubbery on either side of the driveway shrivelled and died.

The sirens were very loud, now. Furth felt the adrenalin begin to drain out of his system. He was beginning to realize that they'd had the .460 Magnum killer cornered and then let him get away. It was Lambert who'd failed to radio for backup, but Furth knew how the system worked. They'd both get tarred with the same brush. Both he and Lambert would spend the next twenty years out on the treadmill of the street, wearing out shoe leather and going nowhere. Disgusted with himself, he tossed the loaded shotgun into the boot. The weapon discharged on impact, blowing a fist-sized hole through the Aspen's rear fender.

The man standing in the rain in his underpants screamed with delight.

XII

THE SNIPER WAS all alone, and he was lonely. He needed human companionship, and he had satisfied his needs by taking an all-night disc jockey to bed with him. The DJ had no talent for conversation, but his voice was rich and soothing and he was very good at monologue.

The sniper lay on his back, the radio nestled in the crook of his arm, a sharp corner digging into his ribs. He was very tired, but couldn't fall asleep. Although he'd adjusted the thermostat as high as it would go before he'd crawled into his sleeping bag, he could still feel the ice in his bones, and every few minutes, without warning, his body would shake with cold, violent, uncontrollable spasms that went on and on, draining him of strength and leaving him feeling weak, exhausted.

He rolled over on his side, hugging himself tight, trying to conserve the heat seeping out of him into the chill air of the apartment. As he moved, his arm brushed against the dial of the radio. The DJ's voice filled with static, became scratchy and indistinct, faded. The sniper didn't notice. He was thinking about the shooting of Andy Patterson, the chase that had followed. He saw himself crouched like an animal at the rear of the underground garage, the garage suddenly filling with a lurid orange light as the stolen Ford exploded in a ball of flame.

It was a lucky thing, the quick police response to the shooting on Jervis Street. If they'd shown up a few minutes later, he had a terrible feeling it would have been too late to save the bald man and his blonde girlfriend.

It had taken an effort of will to ignore the two targets standing frozen in the glass-encased lobby of the apartment. The man and the woman had spoiled his concentration. He'd resented it and even though it would have been an irrational act, had been toying with the idea of killing them both. But he wanted to be sure of Andy Patterson first. Patterson was the primary target.

And then he'd heard it, the faint wail of an approaching siren. A nasty, insistent whine.

There always came a time when everything fell to pieces. Most people knew it but hardly anybody believed it, because if you really believed it, then you had to face the consequences. Luck was all.

The sniper was a pro, but he'd let his rage get the better of him, had loitered far too long at the scene of his crime. He'd wanted to be sure of Patterson. The plan had been to kill him, and the sniper wanted to get it right the first time around.

But he shouldn't have been able to get away. They should have had him cold. He'd been so lucky that he could not stop himself from worrying that he had used up a lifetime of luck all in one moment. He couldn't understand why more police cars hadn't joined the pursuit. There were always seven or eight units in the West End. One call on the radio, and they'd have boxed him in within a few minutes.

As the sniper stared blindly up at the ceiling, a part of his mind began to wonder if he was wrong in assuming that he had managed to get away. What if they knew exactly who he was? What if they were at that very moment deflecting neighbourhood traffic, surrounding the building, slipping quietly into the lobby and elevators, hiding in the stairwells, furtively creeping down the hallways? Dark, featureless men, guns in hand.

The thought grew. Suspicion evolved into certainty. The sniper grabbed the electrical cord and yanked the plug out of the wall, silencing the radio.

At first the only sound he could hear was the sound of his own breathing, shallow and ragged. Then, gradually, he became aware of the distant hum of traffic and then of the almost imperceptible sounds of the building itself, the minute expansions and contractions of concrete and steel, the dull throbbing of unseen engines, whirring of air conditioners, faint hiss of fluorescent tubes.

The rising drone of an elevator.

The sniper reached for the .45 automatic on the floor beside

106

him. His fingers groped through dust and used Kleenex. He found the gun and thumbed back the hammer. Rain slapped against the glass doors leading to the balcony. A gust of wind made the curtains dance. The sniper kicked free of the sleeping bag. He crawled naked across the floor, his eyes on the thin slit of light beneath the door. He heard the elevator doors slide open, muttered conversation. He held his left arm up in front of his face. According to the luminous dials of his watch it was 3:15 a.m. The dead of night — a good time for a surprise assault.

The sniper moved slowly and silently to the door. He eased back the deadbolt, careful not to make the slightest sound, and then used his left hand to turn the knob as far as it would go. Then he raised the .45 to chest level and yanked the door open and rushed outside.

The hallway was empty, deserted. The elevator doors were open but there was no one inside. The sniper stood in a half-crouch, the big automatic clutched in a two-handed grip, his finger on the trigger. Around a turn in the hallway he heard the scratch of a key in a lock and then a burst of laughter, the voice of a woman, loud and shrill. He took three rapid strides down the corridor and then stopped. After a moment he turned and went back into his apartment, slamming the door shut behind him but not bothering to lock it.

The needle of the thermostat was steady at eighty-six degrees. He dropped the pistol on the floor and climbed back into the sleeping bag. His heart thumped against his ribs. His body shook uncontrollably. He shifted into a prenatal position. He had never been colder. His bones were made of ice.

XIII

INSPECTOR BRADLEY, HIS hands clasped behind him, stood at his window and stared out at the harbour. The water was a flat and listless strip of grey. Beyond, the North Shore mountains were obscured by rain and by the same thick, sluggish grey clouds that blanketed the city.

Bradley dropped his gaze to the construction site, almost directly below him. During the week several huge digging machines working sixteen-hour days had chewed a deep hole in the wet clay. On Friday, workmen had sprayed the steeply-pitched sides of the excavation with quick-drying cement. Now, as he watched, a dozen or more labourers lay a complex network of iron reinforcing rods across the bottom of the hole, in preparation for the first pour of concrete. Bradley was no architect, but based on the depth of the foundation, he suspected the finished building was going to be at least twenty storeys high. Soon he would lose his recently acquired ocean view, and his tiny office would sink once more into a state of perpetual twilight.

Massaging his aching temples, he went over to his desk and collapsed into his leather chair. Aside from the usual clutter, the desk was crowded with several plastic or glassine evidence bags containing:

Thirteen spent .460 Magnum cartridges.

Two empty magazines from a Winchester .460 Magnum rifle.

Twenty-three cigarette butts stained with Chinese Red lipstick.

A slightly-worn high-heeled shoe made of white leather, with a heart stitched in red directly above the instep.

One pair of fluffy pink earmuffs.

There was also a glass of lukewarm tap water on the desk, and an empty aspirin bottle. Bradley picked up the aspirin bottle and shook it, then dropped it in his wastepaper basket. He looked at

Franklin, who was sitting hunched on one of the wooden chairs lined up against the wall opposite the desk. "You don't happen to have an aspirin on you, by any chance, do you, George?"

"What?" said Franklin. His voice was hoarse. He sounded as if he'd been taking a little nap. He didn't raise his eyes from the floor.

"I said, you got any aspirin on you?"

Franklin shook his head. He scratched absently at a thin line of dried blood above his upper lip, where he'd cut himself shaving.

An errant gust of wind threw a handful of rain across the window. The fat drops trickled slowly down the glass, cutting erratic paths through the accumulated dust.

"You okay, George?"

"Never better," said Franklin dully.

"You don't have to stay, you know. There's no real reason for you to be here."

Franklin didn't say anything. Bradley decided to let it go. Jerry Goldstein had found Dave Atkinson's prints all over the inside of the walk-in closet in Phasia Palinkas' bedroom, verifying Franklin's version of the events leading up to the shooting. Technically, Franklin was off the hook even though the internal investigation was continuing. But the unofficial thinking was that Franklin had screwed up badly, and that his partner had died as a result. Bradley had dealt with the situation by sticking Franklin behind a desk, making him assistant to Staff Sergeant Peter Yip, who was the case liaison officer. Franklin hadn't been too keen on the job, but Bradley had made it brutally clear it was the only one available to him. Both Atkinson and Franklin had been good cops. Now neither of them were of any use at all. As far as Bradley was concerned, George Franklin had nobody to blame but himself.

A distorted fist hit the pane of frosted glass in Bradley's door, interrupting his chain of thought. The door swung open. Claire Parker walked into the office, and then Jack Willows.

"Have either of you two got an aspirin?" said Bradley.

"I do," said Parker.

"God bless."

Parker rummaged through her purse, handed Bradley a small metal tin.

Bradley popped the tin open and found five dusty white pills inside. He popped two of the pills into his mouth and swallowed half an inch of lukewarm water. When he picked up the water glass it left a pale green ring on the darker green of his desk blotter. He rubbed at the ring with the ball of his thumb. "I guess you two have heard by now that the cabbie died this morning?"

Willows nodded.

Bradley helped himself to another aspirin. "But what I bet you didn't know is that he was a fella of the limp-wristed persuasion."

"He was gay?" said Parker.

"I didn't say he was happy, I said he was a queer." Bradley chased the last two aspirins around the inside of the tin, cornered and ate them, drank some more water. He snapped the lid shut and tossed the tin back to Parker, who caught it one-handed and dropped it into her purse. Bradley pushed the water glass around on his desk. He took the pink earmuffs out of the evidence bag, flexed the steel headband and struck a muscleman's pose. "The point is, we now have a killer who dresses like the Queen of the May, and a victim who's a certified fairy. I don't know about everybody else, but I smell a homosexual angle."

"What about Alice Palm and Phasia Palinkas?" said Parker. "How do they fit in?"

"I thought you'd never ask," said Bradley. He turned to Willows. "There's a woman named Flora McCormick, runs an outfit called the West Coast Singles Club. Alice Palm was a member. So was Andy Patterson."

"What about Phasia Palinkas?" said Parker.

"Let me know what you find out," said Bradley.

Willows started towards the door, but Parker wasn't finished yet. She took a small spiral-bound notebook and a bright yellow ballpoint pen out of her purse, and said, "Where's Flora McCormick's club located, Inspector?"

"In the yellow pages," Bradley replied. "You manage to track down a phone book, you've got it made."

Parker glared at him, then spun on her heel and stormed out of the office, slamming the door behind her. Bradley winced. His headache, despite all the aspirin he'd taken, was absolutely killing him. He tossed the earmuffs down on the desk and said to Franklin, "The girl's got quite a temper, hasn't she, George?"

Franklin didn't give the slightest indication that he was aware that Bradley had spoken to him. He just sat there in his chair, gazing off into space, idly picking at his wound.

Flora McCormick's singles club was located on the main floor of a squat two-storey stucco building in the 500 block West Broadway. Above the entrance a bright red man danced frenetically with a bright blue woman, neon limbs crackling in the rain as they jumped endlessly back and forth.

Parker and Willows walked under the sign and pushed through double glass doors and then made their way down a long, dimly-lit corridor with a highly-polished black linoleum floor. Somewhere ahead of them and off to the left there was the sound of shattering glass, a muffled curse.

Willows broke into a run. Parker hurried after him, her shoes clattering on the linoleum. They passed beneath a curtained archway and into a long, rectangular dining room.

Flora McCormick stood in the middle of a sea of tables, sweeping the last fragments of a wine glass into a metal dustpan. Behind her, at the far end of the room, there was a parquet dance floor and a small raised stage.

Flora McCormick was in her early fifties, about five foot four and one hundred pounds. No heavyweight. Her hair was cut short and combed straight back over a narrow skull. She was wearing cream Hush Puppies and a baggy dark green pant suit that seemed to drain all the colour out of her pale green eyes. Parker was close enough to count the trio of engagement rings crowded together on the third finger of her left hand before Flora heard them coming, and looked up. Parker introduced herself, and then Willows. Flora nodded, and kept working.

"I'll be with you in a few minutes," she said. "Just let me get the rest of these glasses laid out."

There were about fifty tables in the room, four place settings to each table. Only half a dozen of the tables had glasses on them. Parker glanced at Willows. He shrugged, leaving it up to her to

111

decide how to handle the situation. She moved over to one of the cardboard boxes, opened it, and went to work. Willows hesitated, and then followed her lead.

A quarter of an hour later, Flora McCormick led them back down the linoleum hallway and into an office so small that the furniture seemed out of scale. To the left of the door there were two folding metal chairs and a grey metal desk. To the right a row of five steel filing cabinets were lined up against the wall. There were two more cabinets on either side of a tiny window set high in the wall opposite the door. Parker walked over to the window. An aspidistra languished on the sill. She had to stand on her toes to see outside. The view was of a parking lot. At the far end of the lot a man in an idling tow truck was reading a newspaper. It was still raining.

Willows stood on a scrap of carpet in front of the desk while Flora searched through the drawers looking for her keys. Above the filing cabinets, hundreds of black and white photographs covered every available inch of the wall, all the way up to the ceiling. Most of the pictures were framed, but many were not and these had simply been push-pinned to the plaster. All were of past dinners and dances. They had been arranged in chronological order. The oldest picture Willows could find was dated New Year's Eve, 1947. A dark, hairy man wearing oversized diapers and a pointed party hat cavorted on top of one of the round tables in the dining room. A woman had taken the man's cardboard scythe away from him, and was using the sharp point of it to try to pull down his diapers, much to the amusement of the surrounding crowd. 1947. Willows found himself wondering where they all were now.

Flora McCormick eased past him, key ring in hand. She moved to the filing cabinet to the left of the window, unlocked it and slid open the top drawer.

"You always keep the filing cabinets locked?" said Willows.

"I sure do."

"What about the keys, you always keep them in your desk?"

"That's right."

"You ever lock the desk?"

"Not that I can remember." Flora McCormick thumbed

112

through a thick sheaf of straw-coloured folders. "Doesn't make much sense, does it?"

"Not to me," said Willows.

Parker sat down on the edge of the metal desk, glanced idly at the three framed photographs clustered around the telephone.

Flora looked up, smiled fondly. "That's Harry with the cigar. He was the first, and the best. The guy in the glasses, that's Ralph. A bum. Died of cancer of the pancreas eleven years ago. No, make it twelve. Two weeks before his forty-fifth birthday, can you imagine? Cut off in his prime." Flora peered up at Willows, clearly estimating his age, and frowned at what she saw. "The movie star in the turtleneck sweater, that's Bill. My third and last mistake. Look at those teeth. Have you ever seen a nicer smile?" Flora pushed the drawer shut and opened the one beneath it. "The trouble was, Bill never seemed to be smiling at me."

She selected a folder, pulled it out, and handed it to Willows. Alice Palm's name was written on the side in a stylish, spidery hand. Willows flipped open the file. Parker abandoned her perch on the desk to look over his shoulder.

There was very little in the file that was new to Willows, and it contained no information that seemed even potentially useful to him. Alice Palm's date of birth, height, weight, and hair and eye colour were all listed in the same spidery hand that was on the cover of the folder. Her hobbies included the usual eclectic and unlikely mix of sedentary pursuits and violent contact sports. It was obvious that the sole purpose of the list was to give her the widest possible appeal to anyone looking for a woman with similar interests.

The space reserved for religion had been left blank, although Willows knew she'd been an Anglican.

The date on the file indicated that it had been opened five years earlier. Willows doubted that the photograph stapled to the top left-hand corner of the page was less than ten years old.

Flora handed him a second folder. Andy Patterson's name had been pencilled rather than inked on the side flap. His photograph was a Polaroid, and had been taken inside the office, with the door shut so he could stand in front of it. His face and hair had a faint greenish tinge. Willows had seen the effect before: it came of using outdated film.

He read quickly through the short list of Patterson's personal statistics, the notes on his hobbies, his likes and dislikes. Patterson and Alice Palm seemed to have almost nothing in common. While she was a fan of classical music and rock, his preferences were Willie Nelson and jazz.

"What sort of crowd do you get here?" Willows asked Flora McCormick.

"What d'you mean?"

"The people who come here to have a good time, what are they like? I mean age, education, stuff like that."

Flora shrugged. "Most of the people we get here are older than either Alice Palm or Andy Patterson were. But on the other hand, some of them are quite a bit younger." She eased the file drawer shut. "All sorts of people walk in here. You'd be surprised."

"You get many homosexuals?"

Flora nodded. "I thought that's what you were getting at."

"Did Andy Patterson know Alice Palm?"

"I doubt it."

"Did Alice know Phasia Palinkas?"

"I already told your Inspector Bradley that Phasia Palinkas wasn't a member of this club. And the place isn't a gay hangout, either. Patterson was the only homosexual member we've ever had."

"That you know of."

"Right," said Flora McCormick emphatically.

"What was Patterson doing here?"

"He only came two or maybe three times. I think he was trying to figure out which way the wind was blowing."

"How's that again?"

"I don't think he was comfortable with his sexuality. I think he started coming here because it was an easy way to rub shoulders with a lot of women. He wanted to see if he could make it as a heterosexual."

"Interesting theory."

"Can you come up with a better one?"

114

"What about Alice Palm?" said Parker. "What was she doing here?"

Flora smiled wistfully. "Like most of my regulars, she was very nice and very shy. Except for the club, I don't think she had much of a social life."

"How often did she drop by?"

"We have a dinner and dance on Friday and Saturday nights. She almost always came on Fridays."

"But not Saturdays?"

"Never."

"Did she always come alone?"

"Always," said Flora McCormick.

"What about the return trip?" said Willows. "Did she ever take anybody home with her?"

"Every once in a while."

"How often, exactly?"

"I don't know. Two, maybe three times a month."

"What you're saying is that this shy lady took someone home with her two and sometimes three Fridays out of four."

"I don't know where they went."

"She's been a member of your club almost five years," said Willows. "That's a lot of men. How many names can you give me?"

"None, not a single one."

Willows stared coldly at her. "Don't give me that shit," he said softly. "I'll run you in for obstruction, and I'll have the vice squad shut you down."

"It's the truth! During all the time I knew her, she never left with a regular member."

"Wait a minute," said Parker. "What other kind of member is there?"

"Temporary, a one-time admission." Flora McCormick smiled up at Willows. "Let's say you were thinking about joining the club, but you wanted to find out what it was like before you spent your money. All you'd have to do is walk up to the door, fill out a registration card and pay me fifteen dollars. That'd cover dinner, and all the dancing you wanted. But no drinks."

"How many people do that?" asked Parker.

115

"Quite a few. Over the course of a year, hundreds and hundreds."

"How is it," said Willows, "that out of all those faces, you managed to remember Andy Patterson's even though he'd only come to a couple of dances?"

"I already told you, it was because he was homosexual."

"Otherwise you'd have forgotten all about him, is that right?"

"Probably."

"Maybe you don't remember Phasia Palinkas because she only dropped by once or twice."

"Her name isn't in the files."

"All that means is she wasn't a regular member. Maybe she was just a casual, somebody who dropped in from time to time. Do you keep the registration cards your customers fill out when they pay fifteen bucks for a one-nighter?"

"I have to, because of the income tax. I've got them all the way back to 1961, when Harry and I bought the business."

"Where are they?"

"In half a dozen big cardboard boxes in a storage room at the back of the building. You want to see them?"

"Not if I can help it," said Willows. He turned to Parker. "Show her the picture, will you?"

"What picture?" said Flora. She sounded surprised, as if in covering the walls of her office she thought that she had cornered the market.

Parker opened her purse and took out a morgue snap of Phasia Palinkas. The dead woman's eyes were closed, and her face had a peculiarly slack and boneless look. But the colour image was much truer than the grainy, blurred, outdated print that had appeared in the newspapers.

Flora sighed, and took a pair of bifocals out of her jacket pocket. She stared down at the still, quiet face for a long time. Then she took off her glasses and put them away and handed the picture back to Parker.

"I've never seen her before," she said firmly.

"Christ," said Willows, despairing. He gestured at the seven steel cabinets ranged along the walls. "How many files have you got in there?"

"Six thousand, give or take a few."

"Christ," said Willows again. He took the snap of Phasia Palinkas from Parker, and propped it up on the windowsill next to the weeping fig. "Unlock the rest of the cabinets," he said to Flora McCormick.

"You still think she's in there somewhere?"

"She better be."

"You'll be here all night," said Flora. There was more than a hint of satisfaction in her voice, more than a trace of a smile in her eyes.

"You stick around until we're finished," said Willows.

They'd started at eleven o'clock in the morning. At three in the afternoon Willows sent out for chicken sandwiches and coffee. He cleared a small space on Flora McCormick's desk and he and Parker sat down next to each other on the two folding metal chairs. The food was limp and tasteless, and Parker had no appetite. She drank a mouthful of the lukewarm coffee, stretched, and went back to work.

The air in the cramped little office was stale, and smelled of sweat and frustration. Parker's wrists ached. Her fingers felt stiff and clumsy, and stung from paper cuts. She opened another file. A man old enough to be her grandfather smiled confidently up at her through the gap in his teeth. He had outsized ears and a shadowy, uneven moustache. Rimless glasses, hardly any hair. Parker shut his file and put it to one side, opened the next.

Her hair had been much longer when the picture was taken, falling to her shoulders and out of frame. She was smiling. The camera's flash had left pinpoints of light in her dark and solemn eyes. A gold cross hung from a thin chain around her neck. Parker stepped away from the filing cabinet, savouring the moment. She waved the file at Willows. He looked up, and then came over to her.

"She registered under the name of Sharon Hopkins," said Parker. She frowned. "Wasn't that the name of one of the other tenants in her apartment block?"

Willows nodded. "The next-door neighbour."

"I wonder why she didn't use her own name."

117

"That makes two of us," said Willows. He went back to the desk, tossed the remains of their lunch into Flora McCormick's wicker wastebasket, and laid the three files down on the desk in a neat row.

Alice Palm.

Phasia Palinkas.

Andy Patterson.

"All three victims were Caucasian," he said. "They were under fifty years of age and their last names all started with the sixteenth letter of the alphabet. Now let's find out what else they had in common."

Parker picked up Andy Patterson's file and began to read, taking it one word at a time.

Two hours later, she had memorized all three files and all she had to show for her labour was a five-star headache. Her purse was on top of the filing cabinet to the left of the window. She opened it and discovered that Bradley had helped himself to every last one of her aspirins.

Seething with anger, she stared at the picture on the wall directly in front of her.

This picture, unlike all the others, was mounted in an ornate oval frame. It had been taken in the dining room down the hall. Parker could see tiny sections of the parquet dance floor through a forest of ankles. The photographer, she thought as her rage gradually subsided, must have crouched and taken the picture from a height of no more than two or three feet. It was a very odd picture indeed, and as Parker studied it she became aware that it was much too small for the space allotted to it on the otherwise crowded wall. She examined it more carefully, and saw that it was the only picture in the room that didn't have a fine coating of dust on top of the frame.

She willed herself to relax, to let her eyes wander over the print, to stop looking and start seeing. The photograph was dated 25th December 1966. The writing was scrawled right across a pair of white high-heeled shoes with decorative hearts stitched above the arches. They were, Parker immediately realized, a perfect mate for the shoe the killer had abandoned on Jervis Street less than twenty-four hours earlier. She'd check with Flora

118

McCormick, but there was no doubt in her mind that the killer had planted the picture in the office, hung it there for her and Willows to find.

It was impossible, but undeniable. The .460 Magnum killer was playing with them, leading them on.

XIV

THE ROOM WAS small, filled with cigar smoke and a dozen dilapidated chairs, a portable projector and a screen that had been mended with wide strips of white adhesive tape filched from a first-aid kit. Mel Dutton finished threading film into the machine as Willows came in through the door.

"Douse the lights, will you, Jack."

"Sure," said Willows. He nodded a greeting to the trio of vice cops lounging in the front-row seats, and flicked the switch. A shaft of light cut through the smoke. Numbers flashed wildly across the screen, followed by the film's credits. Willows didn't recognize any of the names. Dutton adjusted the focus. They were in a house, in a large and modern kitchen. There was no sound track.

"This is genuine Art," said Dutton to Willows. "Film as Literature. I know you're going to be impressed."

There were two girls in the kitchen, sitting opposite each other at a butcher's block table, profiles to the camera. The table had been set for breakfast. There was a four-slice toaster, a loaf of sliced wholewheat bread, a large box of Nabisco Shreddies, glasses, plates and bowls, a salt and pepper set in the shape of windmills.

Willows guessed the girls' ages at fifteen or maybe sixteen, although they had been made up to look even younger. Both girls were blonde, their hair styled in a severe military cut, and lightly streaked in red and green. They were identically dressed in skin-tight pastel sleeveless T-shirts, black satin bikini panties and translucent plastic sandals. Both were smoking.

Behind the table there was a door leading to the back porch, and every few seconds one of the girls would turn and look expectantly at it. Willows had the impression they'd been coached to try to look nervous and excited.

120

"Guess who's coming to breakfast!" said Mel Dutton in a Bill Cosby voice. One of the vice cops chuckled briefly. Another yawned. The third seemed to have fallen asleep.

The camera dollied in, and Willows saw that the girls had their names glitter-printed on the T-shirts across their breasts.

Annie mashed her cigarette out in her cereal and was silently but vigorously chastised by Dewey.

The camera cut erratically to an electric clock on the wall above the sink. A dozen seconds ticked slowly by. Annie lit another cigarette and tossed her match into Dewey's bowl. The cereal caught immediately, burning with a bright orange flame.

"A quality production," said Dutton. "Absolutely first-class values. You notice the lighting?"

"I noticed it right away," said Willows.

Dutton grinned, teeth flashing in the light from the projector.

Dewey used her spoon to extinguish the burning Shreddies. Suddenly she and Annie jumped up and ran to the back door.

"Knock, knock," said Dutton.

Annie got to the door first, yanked it open. A huge black in a milkman's uniform smiled down at her. He was carrying a dozen quarts of milk in a metal rack. Grinning, he allowed himself to be pulled into the kitchen.

Willows noticed he had to duck his head when he came through the doorway.

"The guy's name is LeRoy Johnson," said Dutton. "A failed basketball player. Almost made centre for the Sonics. The club said they couldn't sign him because he was too tall to play, but I hear drugs might have had something to do with it."

On the screen, Annie unbuttoned LeRoy's uniform jacket and discovered to her surprise that he wasn't wearing a shirt. LeRoy tore the cap off a quart of milk, brought the bottle to his mouth and drank thirstily, white rivulets pouring down his muscular, hairless chest.

Dewey was on her knees, working on the wide studded leather belt holding up LeRoy's twill pants. Drops of milk fell across her face. She licked her lips, her eyes sparkling with simulated lust.

Willows squinted through the smoky gloom at the feeder reel on the projector.

121

"Another twenty minutes," said Dutton, his sharp photographer's eye missing nothing.

Willows held up his little package, and pointed at the door leading to Dutton's darkroom.

"What's the matter," said Dutton, "you don't want to find out what happens next?"

"I have a feeling I already know."

Dutton nodded. "Art imitates Life, and Life imitates Art. But most of all, Art imitates Art."

None of the vice cops looked up when Dutton and Willows left the room. Slouching ponderously in the gutted ruins of the upholstered chairs, heavy-lidded, consumed by their own dark and formless shadows, they stared bleakly at the screen and the mute tangle of bodies that squirmed and wriggled on the milk-slippery kitchen floor.

There was an old round-top fridge in the darkroom, used by Dutton to store undeveloped film. He opened the door and reached deep inside, came up with two bottles of Kokanee beer. He popped the electric blue caps and handed a bottle to Willows.

"What are we drinking to this time, Mel?"

"Reincarnation. The possibility that next time around I'll be a seven-foot hunk with a full head of hair."

"Instead of an aphid?"

"Listen, if I'm a nice guy during my current life, there's no problem with regression. So what can I do for you that'll improve my Karma?"

Willows showed him the photograph Claire Parker had found in Flora McCormick's office.

"I heard you fellas did an awful lot of leg work," Dutton cracked, "but I had no idea I was supposed to take the job description so literally."

"Can you enlarge that for me?"

"How many times?"

"I'd like about a dozen copies."

"No, I mean how big do you want it?"

"As big as possible."

Dutton sank half his beer. "You looking for something in particular?"

"Whatever I can find."

Dutton frowned. "To maintain any degree of clarity, I'm going to have to make an interneg. That means photographing your picture, developing the negative and using it to make a series of prints at various exposure levels."

"Sounds complicated."

"Everything's complicated. Until you break it down into its component parts. Then everything all of a sudden becomes ridiculously simple. Which is why we do our best to lead such complicated lives." He tapped the bottom right-hand corner of the photograph. "These shoes with the little hearts, they're the same as the shoe that was left on Jervis, am I right?"

"Could be, Mel."

"This guy you're after, he's killed what, four people?"

"So far," said Willows.

"Point taken," said Dutton, and drained his beer.

A little over an hour later, Dutton pulled the last of the enlargements out of the flatbed drier. Willows went over the print inch by inch while Dutton stood anxiously by.

"You find anything, Jack?"

"No, not yet."

Dutton scowled. His good deed for the day appeared to have been wasted, he hadn't racked up a single Karma point on that big scoreboard in the sky. Who was it that had said the road to being an aphid was paved with good intentions? Shit, he was no closer to a perfect rematerialization than if he'd spent the morning watching drool movies with his pals from vice.

Inspector Bradley stuck his cigar in his mouth and used the flat of his hands to push open the metal fire door. He hurried down a short flight of concrete stairs, bubbling grey paint sloughing off under his heels. Parker, a little out of breath, managed to stay right behind him. A counterweight rattled on the end of a length of rusty chain. The door slammed shut.

Parker's irises shrank before her advancing pupils as her eyes adjusted to the gloom. They were somewhere in the basement of 312 Main, following a sparse string of naked low-wattage bulbs that dwindled into the distance in a perfectly straight line.

Off to her left, somewhere in the darkness, water dripped on metal.

Bradley paused under the third lightbulb in the string. His breathing was fast and shallow, and the film of perspiration on his forehead made his skin look freshly lacquered. Ever since they'd left his office, they'd been walking so fast that Parker had been forced at frequent intervals to break into a trot in order to keep up. She was pleased to see that the rapid pace had also taken its toll on Bradley.

Leaning towards her, he took her gently by the arm. They were so close that she could smell the thin scent of his aftershave under the burly pungency of his cigar. He smiled, but even in the dim and murky light she could see that his eyes were not twinkling.

"You know where I'm going?" he said quietly.

Parker shook her head.

"City Hall. Superintendent Foster and I have an appointment with His Honour the Mayor. And to tell you the truth, I'm not looking forward to it at all. Because voices are bound to be raised. Many rhetorical and some pointed questions will be asked. And if I don't want to get my shoes scuffed, I'm going to have to come up with some hard answers."

They started walking again, into alternating pools of darkness and light.

Bradley indicated the green plastic folder Parker was carrying under her arm. "Franklin tells me you've been a very busy lady. Does that contain the fruits of your labour?"

"Mine and everybody else's," said Parker. There were a dozen clerks working on Flora McCormick's files, putting together a master list of the more than six thousand past and present members of the singles club. The names were being fed into the department's IBM mainframe computer in blocks of one hundred. So far, about two thousand names had been processed. Of these, fifty-three men and eight women had been found to have previous convictions. Parker explained to Bradley that only twelve of the men and one of the women had been involved in crimes of violence.

"That's fine," said Bradley. "Thirteen is a number the Mayor can understand, it's a number he can deal with." He held out his hand and Parker gave him the green file. "These people are our primary suspects," said Bradley. "I want all thirteen of them brought in for questioning, and I want it done right this minute. See Franklin about it. Tell him it's a top priority item."

"Yes, sir."

Bradley tapped the file with a tobacco-stained finger. "Exactly what have I got in here?"

"Names, rap-sheets and mug shots. A selection of crime-scene photographs. A list of the physical evidence."

Bradley nodded, apparently satisfied. "I'll never know why, but His Honour always gets a big kick out of looking at mug shots." As he spoke, Bradley abruptly veered left, down a narrow, dimly lit corridor. "You got anything else for me, or is that it?"

"That's it for now," said Parker. As far as she knew, Willows was still up in the lab with Mel Dutton. Until she found out if they'd come up with something, she saw no point in telling Bradley about the photograph they'd taken from Flora McCormick's office.

They turned left again. Parker smelled burning oil, steam. Bradley stopped in front of another metal fire door. He fiddled with a steel bolt. The bolt was rusty and made a harsh grating sound as he pulled it back. The door swung open, flooding them in soft grey light.

They stepped outside, into cooler air, a sloping, feathery rain. They were in the alley at the rear of 312 Main, standing opposite the police parking lot. Bradley jumped a puddle, strode across an open expanse of asphalt and past an untidy row of police vehicles. The squad car Furth had shot up two days earlier was parked at the far end of the lot. Next to it was Bradley's shiny white Chrysler. He unlocked the car and got in, tossing the green folder on the seat beside him.

Parker stood in the rain, waiting to be dismissed.

Bradley started the Chrysler's engine. He leaned forward in the seat, his chin propped on the steering wheel, and listened intently to the sound of the motor. After a moment he turned to Parker and said, "Automatic choke's giving me a little trouble.

Won't run steady when it's cold. I keep meaning to take it in, but where am I going to find the time?"

Parker smiled sympathetically, and turned up the collar of her jacket against the rain.

"You ought to realize," said Bradley, "that at the moment you happen to be in a unique and enviable position. This is your first homicide, and its turned into a real headline grabber. Very high profile, the sort of case that could make your career."

Parker nodded but said nothing, knowing there was more to come.

"But you're going to have to watch your every step," said Bradley, "because somebody's going to be watching every step you take."

"I understand," said Parker.

"The lowest rung on the ladder is the one that gets stepped on the most," said Bradley. He gave the Chrysler some gas, and frowned. "A police department is a lot like an automobile engine. To make it run efficiently, you have to have all the parts working together to the maximum of their potential. Jack Willows is a hell of a talented cop, but that's something he tends to forget, that we all have to work together." Bradley revved the engine again. It idled smoothly and quietly.

"I appreciate your concern," said Parker.

"Good," said Bradley. He leaned across the seat towards her, reaching out, and for a moment Parker thought his intention was to shake hands. But all he'd wanted was to shut the Chrysler's door. Parker retreated a step as the big car lurched forward. She watched it pick up speed as Bradley drove diagonally across the lot towards the exit.

The rain was falling more heavily now, hissing on the asphalt and in the wide, shallow puddles. Parker turned on her heel and started back towards the station house.

A dark green Impala pulled into the lot, George Franklin hunched myopically over the wheel. He waved at Parker and gave her a big, sloppy grin. She waved back at him, and slowed her pace. Franklin parked the Impala in the space vacated by Bradley. He got out of the car and slammed the door shut, hurried towards Parker. His raincoat hung on him like a shroud,

126

and as he came closer, Parker saw that his face was thin and pale, his eyes sunk deep in shadow.

"Haven't seen you for a couple of days," said Franklin. "You hear the news?"

"What news is that?" said Parker.

"Internal Investigations finally decided I hadn't been such a bad boy after all. Decided to let me keep my little gold badge. Suggested we all get together sometime for a couple of beers. Handshakes all around. A pat on my back."

"I'm glad you're off the hook," said Parker.

"So am I," said Franklin. "So was the little woman." He splashed through a puddle without seeming to notice. "We just had lunch at Puccini's. A celebration. You ever have lunch at Puccini's?"

Parker smiled, shook her head. "Was it a good lunch, George?"

"Terrific. Very tasty."

"What did you eat?"

"Numerous martinis. Some kind of green-coloured pasta. Bottle of white wine. Tomato salad. A couple of liqueurs to finish." It was an effort for Franklin to climb the steps leading to the rear entrance of 312 Main. He reached for the door handle and missed by a foot. Staggering, he bumped his head against the wire-mesh glass.

Parker heard him giggle, saw him wipe a tear from his eye.

He tried the door again, and this time managed to get it open. Standing to one side, he waved Parker into the building. As she walked past him, she noticed a small patch of stubble under his chin, a bevelled cut high up on his cheek. She had a sudden, vivid image of him standing at his morning mirror with his razor in his hand. Full of remorse, trembling, barely under control. Listening with one ear to the little woman down in the kitchen, patiently making a breakfast her husband would not eat.

Franklin had managed to keep his badge, but when Dave Atkinson had died, Franklin had lost something a lot more important than a shiny piece of tin. As they walked down the hallway together, Franklin trailing a cloud of alcohol fumes, Parker wondered if there was any way he could ever get it back.

XV

THE ROSE & THISTLE was crowded, hot, and very, very noisy. Norman Tate, Ron Moore, and Terry Foster were sitting at a corner table with a view of the dart boards, the bar, and the door to the ladies' washroom.

But the subject wasn't darts or women, it was hockey. For the past half hour Foster and Moore had been exchanging Wayne Gretzky anecdotes, making snaking motions in and out of the clutter of empty glasses on the table as they took turns describing yet another miraculous rush up ice.

Tate scowled into his beer. He was bored and he was restless, verging on irritable. Leaning back in his chair, sipping from his glass, he regarded his two friends with that special degree of fond acrimony accessible only to drunks.

Foster could have been Moore's brother, and he, Tate, might have been kin to either of them. All three could have been brothers. Triplets. Of course, Moore's complexion was a little on the dark side, and Foster had lost most of his hair. But all three men were in their early thirties, average height, a few pounds overweight. They were all single and determined to stay that way. And despite the amount of skull Foster was showing, all three continued to look two or three years younger than their actual age.

Why was that, exactly? Suddenly, without consciously thinking about it, Tate had the answer. It had nothing to do with being young at heart, the luck of the genetic draw, magic. It was an excess of fat and a lack of ambition that had, so far, managed to keep the lines and wrinkles of old age at bay.

Tate's heart ached.

Smoke got in his eyes.

He drained his beer, slammed the empty glass down on the table and yelled, "Shit!" into one of those freakish glades of silence that, from time to time, inexplicably occur. Every female within a twenty-foot radius turned towards him, glaring. This is no rowdy hotel bar, those sleek and youthful faces reproached.

The waitress, standing at an adjoining table, gave Tate a look of bleak revulsion. His eyes wandered over her gold lamé jumpsuit, which she must surely have climbed into one thread at a time. He smiled, and gave her the finger. Turning, she tried to catch the bouncer's eye. In a few short seconds, Tate was the only male in the bar who wasn't looking at her. Responding to her audience, her gestures became less hectic, more graceful and theatrical.

Tate leaned over and helped himself to a beer from her tray, tipped her with a pinch.

The bouncer started towards them, taking a straight line through the crowd. Tate watched him through the sudsy bottom of his glass, marvelling at the way he seemed to double in volume with every stride he took.

He looked at his watch. It was getting late, it was time to leave.

Foster dropped a five-dollar bill on the table, timing it perfectly. The waitress swooped down like a shapely, golden vulture. The bouncer, in order to avoid knocking her flat, was forced to swerve sharply to his left. He hit a chair and knocked it over, lost his balance and threw out an arm to steady himself. Knocked a rye and ginger into a customer's lap.

Moore was first out the door. Foster was right behind him. Tate brought up the rear.

It was raining, but only just. A gentle wind drifted up the street from the harbour, half a mile away. The air smelled of salt and mercurocrome. Tate belched and said, "Where's your car, Moore?"

Moore lifted his nose and sniffed the air, pointed towards a multi-storey parking lot at the far end of the block.

"There's no way I can make it that far on foot," said Foster. "Somebody's gonna have to call a cab."

"Walk or die," said Moore.

Tate belched again.

"That reminds me," said Foster, "I'm hungry. After we get the car, let's drive over to the Fresgo and grab a burger and a brew."

"Good idea," said Tate.

"Let's do it anyway," said Moore.

Moore's dark green Triumph TR3 convertible was parked on the fifth level of the lot, sandwiched between a silver Cadillac and a dark blue Buick. Moore rapped his knuckles on the roof of the Caddy. "Detroit shit comes in big lumps," he said, and eased down into the soft leather bucket-seat of the Triumph.

Tate beat Foster to the single passenger seat by a half-step. Foster gave Tate a sneer as he wedged himself sideways into the small space between the seats and the rear deck of the car.

Moore slipped on a pair of black leather racing gloves, flexed his hands, and jammed an undersized tweed hat on his head. The hat gave him an obtrusive, ferrety look. He patted himself down, found his keys and started the engine.

Tate made a show of fastening his seatbelt.

"Fuck off," said Moore, "I taught Mario Andretti everything he knows."

"That's the Mario Andretti who tends bar over at the Phoenix," said Foster.

Moore adjusted his rearview mirror, smiled at Foster's reflection. "You comfy back there?"

"No."

"Good." Moore lit a cheap cigar, flicked the burning match out on to the oil-stained concrete. He put the car in gear, red-lined the engine and popped the clutch. The rear end dipped and the little car shot forward. Moore spun the wheel, and they slewed sideways towards the exit ramp. He shifted into second gear and they powered through the descending spiral tunnel, the rich clamour of the exhaust reverberating off the concrete walls.

Foster hung on tight as they rocketed around the final turn and down the straight towards the Richards Street exit. He braced himself against the back of Tate's seat as Moore took his foot off the gas and let the transmission and high compression engine work to slow their approach to the small, white-painted collection booth. Moore tapped the brakes, and the Triumph stopped opposite the booth.

The attendant's sliding window was shut tight. It was made of plexiglass that was badly scratched and yellow with age. Foster saw a shadowy figure move inside. A hand pressed against the plexiglass and then fell away.

Tate watched Moore search through his pockets, frown, glance at the dashboard and then at the floor of the car.

"What is it, you lose your parking ticket again?"

"Just misplaced it," said Moore. His cigar clenched firmly between his teeth, he leaned across Tate and flipped open the glove compartment. The Triumph's insurance and registration papers were crammed in there, along with maps of the province, Washington state and California. Under the maps Moore found a wrinkled apple, a handful of Chevron receipts, a pen that didn't work and a battered paperback copy of a bestseller he'd never read.

But no parking ticket.

Which meant he was going to have to do some fast talking or pay the maximum day rate: triple the amount he actually owed. He slammed the glove compartment shut and turned towards the collection booth.

The attendant had opened the plexiglass window, and he was watching them. He had clear blue eyes, and he was crying. Tears streamed down his coarse and stubbled cheeks, smearing his thickly applied makeup.

Moore blinked. There was too much to take in at once. His focus shifted from the cheap blonde wig to the violent slash of bright red lipstick that angled across the mouth and over the left nostril.

The man turned to face Moore more squarely. The lace trim of his white dress rippled, and then lay still.

Moore disengaged the clutch. He shifted from neutral to first gear.

The barrel of the Winchester came up. Moore saw himself in miniature, his fear reflected in the polished lens of the Redfield scope.

He started to let in the clutch.

There was a deafening explosion, a scorching flash of light. Five hundred grains of copper-jacketed lead alloy punched a hole in him the size of a grapefruit, killing him instantly. His foot slipped off the clutch. The Triumph crawled forward a few feet, and then the engine coughed and died.

Tate stared uncomprehendingly down at the corpse lying across his lap. The huge wound in Moore's back was streaming. The inside of the car was splattered with gouts of blood, chunks of flesh, startlingly white splinters of bone.

Tate screamed. He tried without success to push Moore away from him. A piece of Moore's shirt came free in his hands. There was blood all over him. He tried to stand up, and was contained by the seatbelt. Clawing at the corpse, struggling to free himself from Moore's sticky embrace, Tate bared his teeth and shrieked with frustration, rage and fear.

Foster scrambled to his feet and twisted to face the rear of the car. Richards Street was less than twenty feet away. If he hit the concrete on the run, the killer would have time to fire no more than a single hurried shot. And he'd still have Tate to worry about. Would he choose the moving target instead of taking the easy shot? Foster didn't think so. He got a foot up on the Triumph's sloping trunk, and jumped.

The bullet caught him on the wing, at the apex of his flight. It smashed his hip bone and deflected upwards to plough a vertical path through his stomach wall, eviscerating him with all the force and delicacy of a blunt axe.

He hit the concrete face down. There was a third shot, but he didn't hear it.

132

XVI

WILLOWS LAY ON the Chesterfield with an arm flung across his face to fend off the flickering light of the television. On the coffee table in front of the Chesterfield there was an empty highball glass and an old Hardy split-cane flyrod. Willows had spent much of the evening drinking Scotch, retying the rod's guides and ferrules, carefully cutting away and replacing worn thread with new, applying a thin layer of clear varnish. At eleven o'clock he'd turned on the television to watch the news. Now, at twenty past, Pamela Martin was reporting on an East End warehouse that had gone up in smoke, and Willows was sleeping soundly.

The telephone rang fifteen times before the harsh jangling finally penetrated Willows' consciousness, his restless dreams. He yawned, stretched, and his outflung arm knocked over the empty highball glass. The tip of the Hardy quivered.

Willows got up and turned off the television, hurried down the short hallway to the bedroom. The telephone was on the night table beside the bed. He picked it up on the nineteenth ring.

"Jack?" It was Inspector Bradley. He sounded as if he'd run out of indigestion tablets a long time ago.

"What happened?" said Willows. His voice was hoarse with sleep. He coughed, clearing his throat.

"We've had another shooting. A multiple."

"Where?"

"A parking lot, over on Richards."

"What's the address, Inspector?"

Bradley sighed wearily into the phone. "It happened an hour ago, Jack. The party's moved across town, to the morgue."

"I'll be there in twenty minutes."

Bradley hung up.

Willows sat on the edge of the bed with the phone in his lap, staring down at the silver-framed photograph of Jean, Mickey,

133

and Laura. The picture had been taken the previous July, at a backyard barbecue. Jean was in shorts, a halter top. The kids had been splashing in the plastic pool and were wearing matching Speedo bathing suits. Willows missed them more than he cared to admit, even to himself. A month ago, Jean had announced without warning that she'd bought three Air Canada tickets to Toronto. She was going to spend some time with her parents, decide what to do with her marriage. She was taking the children.

Willows had left her alone for a week, then called on the telephone. She hadn't been pleased to hear from him, and he hadn't called again, deciding that the best thing to do was to do nothing but sit quietly, and wait, and hope.

The city morgue, with its pale orange brick façade and white mullioned windows, is located on Cordova Street, just around the corner from 312 Main. The first and second floors were dark, but there was light leaking from the windows up on the top floor, where the cutting was done.

Willows parked his Oldsmobile next to a fire hydrant. He locked the car and hurried, shoulders hunched against the rain, across the sidewalk and around to the rear of the building. A wide asphalt driveway provided ambulance access from the lane to the service elevator. Willows stepped into the elevator and pushed the UP button. The doors slid shut and an overhead fan rattled noisily. Drops of water fell from the hem of Willows' coat to the bare metal floor. He wiped the rain from his face, and put his wife and children out of his mind.

The elevator jerked to a stop. The doors slid open and the fan rattled and died. Willows walked down a long, unusually wide corridor and then pushed through double swing doors into the operating theatre. Claire Parker was leaning against the wall next to a window overlooking the lane. The window was open. Parker was getting a breath of fresh air. Willows said hello, and she gave him a wan smile.

The operating theatre was a large, perfectly square, brightly lit room. The floor and two walls were covered with small, glossy blue tiles. The other walls were lined with refrigerated stainless steel drawers resembling huge filing cabinets. Two zinc tables

134

stood directly beneath a massive cast-iron and frosted glass skylight, a faintly glowing, distorted slice of moon. Each table was seven feet long and three feet wide, and stood exactly forty-two inches above the tiled floor. A constant stream of cold water ran across the tops of the tables and down chrome drainage pipes that vanished into the tiles. Norman Tate's body lay on the nearest of the tables, concealed by a bloody lime-green sheet.

Inspector Bradley leaned against the other table. His hands were in his pockets and there was an unlit cigar clenched in his unhappy mouth. He glanced up as Willows entered the room, and then his eyes drifted back to the lime-green sheet.

The pathologist, Christy Kirkpatrick, stood at a sink with his back to Willows. The water was running hard, splashing in the basin. Something glinted in Kirkpatrick's large, freckled hands. He shut off the water, dried his hands on a threadbare white towel. Turning, he saw Willows and gave him a cheerful smile.

"How goes it, Jack?"

"You tell me," said Willows.

Kirkpatrick folded the towel and hung it up, taking his time. He was a large, loose-limbed man in his early sixties, with pale blue eyes and the complexion of a cherub. Despite his age, he had something of a reputation as a rake. There was a long-standing rumour, unsubstantiated but persistent, that he'd ended an affair with Superintendent Ford's wife only a week before she'd initiated divorce proceedings against her husband.

Bradley took the dead cigar out of his mouth. He lifted the lime-green sheet.

Willows took a look, and said, "Who was he?"

"His name's Norman Tate."

Willows said to Parker, "Was he a member of Flora McCormick's club?"

Parker nodded. She looked cold, but she was staying close to the window.

Willows turned back to Bradley. "Why wasn't I called before the bodies were moved? Why did you wait more than an hour before you phoned me?"

"Don't blame me, Jack. George Franklin was supposed to take care of it. Maybe you should talk to him."

"If I can sober him up long enough to get a straight answer out of him."

"The man's taking it hard, Jack. Can you blame him?"

Willows made an impatient gesture of dismissal. "You said it was a multiple murder. How many bodies have we got?"

"Three. The other two are in the basement of the General, waiting for an autopsy. I had this one brought over here because there was no exit wound, and that isn't consistent with the pattern."

"Neither is a triple shooting."

Kirkpatrick walked towards them, his crêpe soles making little sucking noises on the tiles. He handed Bradley a battered rifle bullet. The misshapen chunk of metal reflected light as Bradley turned it over and over in his hand.

"Four-sixty Magnum," said Willows.

"Retrieved only after a long and arduous search," said Kirkpatrick.

"Why wasn't there an exit wound?" said Bradley.

"Nothing tricky about that," said Kirkpatrick. He grasped a corner of the lime-green sheet and flung it dramatically back, exposing the naked corpse from head to toe.

"That's the entrance wound right there, just to the left of the sternum."

Kirkpatrick's finger hovered over the mutilated, badly bruised flesh. Willows noticed that the fingernail was bitten to the quick. Kirkpatrick traced the twisting, convoluted path taken by the bullet.

"The bullet penetrated the upper left part of the heart and the left lung. It then deflected off the eighth thoracic vertebra, passing through the diaphragm and abdominal muscles, sliced down through the thigh parallel to the bone, and finally came to rest below the lower end of the femur."

"Could we have that in layman's language?" said Bradley.

Kirkpatrick smiled benignly. "The bullet bounced around inside the guy like he was a human pinball machine, and ran out of juice behind his knee. He was shot and killed."

"There was no particular reason that the bullet stayed inside the body?"

136

"A weird flight path, that's all."

"Why were you in such a rush to dig out the bullet?" Willows asked Bradley.

"I wanted to make sure we were dealing with the same shooter, not a copy-cat. The other two bullets hit concrete and disintegrated. They were too broken up to make a comparison."

"Why not compare the brass, check out the ejector marks?"

"There was no brass," said Bradley. He chewed on his cigar, spat out a shred of tobacco. "That's what aggravates me, Jack. That there were three shootings, instead of one. That only one of the victims was a member of the singles club. And that there wasn't any brass left at the crime scene. The pattern's been broken, and it bothers me. That's why I wanted the bullet, so I could get it down to the lab and stick it under a spectroscope and make damn sure it came from the same gun that killed the first four victims. Because if it didn't, we're in real serious trouble."

Willows held up his hands, palms out. "Okay, okay. I was just asking. Didn't the killer leave anything behind?"

"Half a roast beef sandwich with a big bite out of it. A plastic container of coleslaw."

"We can get a blood type from the saliva on the sandwich."

"If we're lucky." Bradley spat another shred of tobacco. "There were prints all over the lid of the coleslaw container."

"Retrievable prints?"

"Goldstein seems to think so."

"Our witnesses have the killer wearing white cotton gloves."

"Don't be a pessimist, Jack. Pessimists go home early and sleep in late. I only want winners on my team."

"So do I," said Willows. "If George Franklin screws up again, I want him off the case. I mean right out of it, I don't want him even keeping track of the paper clips. And I don't give a damn how he feels about it, understand?"

"Sure," said Bradley.

Willows started the Olds and turned on the heater and windscreen wipers. Parker sat quietly on the far side of the seat, staring out through the glass at the rain drumming down on the hood of the car. Willows switched on the lights and released the

137

emergency brake. He made a wide U-turn and then a left on Main, drove two blocks and swung right on Pender, down the gently sloping hill that bisected the heart of Chinatown — or at least the Chinatown the tourists knew about. The dozens of restaurants were closed and dark, but there were lights glowing dimly on the top floor of several of the taller buildings. Illegal mah-jong games, probably. Every two or three years the department made a highly publicized attempt to shut the games down, but the raids were more a public relations gesture than an attempt to end the gambling. In 1887, the Chinese had built a high wooden fence from Shanghai Alley across to Canton Alley. The fence had been built to safeguard the population from attacks by hostile whites, and in a sense it had never come down. There were more than a hundred thousand Chinese in the metropolitan area, and only four of them were members of the police force. The community policed itself. It always had, and likely always would.

Willows stopped for a red light at the corner of Pender and Homer. He watched a fat man in striped coveralls conduct a delicate investigation into the soggy contents of a fire-blackened litter bin. The man came up with an empty Pepsi bottle. He caught Willows' eye, and grinned a toothless grin.

The light changed. Willows turned left, south on Homer. The heater was working now, and he switched the fan on to maximum. A blast of warm air flooded across his legs. He glanced over at Parker. She was sitting bolt upright with her hands clenched firmly in her lap, staring straight ahead.

"Are you all right?" he said quietly.

No response.

He reached out and gently touched her arm. She turned slowly towards him and gave him an odd look, an off-balanced look, as if she couldn't quite remember who he was.

Willows pointed at the glove compartment. "There's a bottle in there. Would you mind getting it out for me?"

Parker thought about it for a moment, and then nodded. She opened the glove compartment and a mickey of Cutty Sark tumbled into her lap. Wordlessly, she passed the bottle to Willows. He broke the seal and unscrewed the cap, passed the

138

bottle back to her. She lifted the bottle to her lips, sipped delicately.

At Granville Street, Willows was forced to stop and wait for a break in the traffic. Parker's hair, backlit by red neon, looked as if it was on fire.

A bus shot past in the opposite lane, throwing up a huge sheet of dirty grey water. Parker handed the Scotch to Willows. He sipped companionably, and handed it back. She helped herself to another hefty shot. He watched her throat move as she swallowed. The lines of tension around her mouth and eyes seemed a little less deep now, and there was a hint of colour in her skin.

Willows made his left, heading towards the Granville Street bridge. They were more than halfway across the bridge when Parker finally started talking.

"Two of them were in the car. The other one was lying on the concrete beside the car. He was curled up on his side, as if he was asleep. I've never seen so much blood. There was blood everywhere I looked. I could smell it. I can smell it now."

Willows took the Fourth Avenue off-ramp. He was driving automatically, all his attention on Parker, and he almost failed to see the girl walking against the light at the corner of Fourth and Burrard. Cursing, he hit the brakes and leaned on the horn. The girl didn't look up. The big Oldsmobile skidded across the wet asphalt and came to a stop inches from her right hip.

The girl was fifteen or maybe sixteen years old. She was wearing a black leather jacket and tight black leather pants, black leather boots. A miniature poodle trailed along behind her on a silver chain. The dog was black, and it was wearing a black leather tuxedo jacket.

Despite the rain, the girl was not carrying an umbrella or wearing a hat. Her long black hair was matted to her scalp, lay in thick strands across her pale face. The girl peered intently in through the windshield of the Oldsmobile. Parker saluted her with the bottle. The girl smiled, waved, and tugged hard on the silver chain. The poodle yelped shrilly, got up on its hind legs and performed a spirited little dance across the intersection. Willows saw that the animal's tuxedo was studded with sequins and imitation pearls. Then the light changed from green to amber

139

and he was spinning the wheel, gunning the Olds straight up Burrard to Eleventh, where he braked hard and made a left.

Parker's apartment was in the middle of the block. The lawn needed mowing. The gold letters on the door were beginning to flake away. Willows pulled up to the curb and turned off his lights, but left the engine running.

Parker screwed the metal cap back on the bottle and put the bottle in her coat pocket. She gave Willows a sad, brittle smile, and opened her door. "Thanks for the ride."

"Anytime," said Willows.

She patted her pocket. The bottle gurgled. "I guess I owe you a drink."

"Forget it." Willows hesitated, and then said, "Are you going to be okay?"

Parker shook her head. "No, as a matter of fact, I don't think I am."

"Want some company?"

"I don't know. Probably not."

Parker got out of the car and slammed the door shut. Willows sat there for a moment, both hands on the wheel, watching her walk slowly towards her apartment. Then, with a quick, decisive movement, he reached out and turned the key in the ignition, killing the engine.

In the mirrored lobby, they had to wait a long time for the elevator. Parker rested her head on Willows' shoulder, but kept her hands in her pockets. He watched his reflected image put his arms around her. Neither of them seemed to have much to say. The elevator arrived. They stepped inside. Parker pushed the button for the third floor.

Up they went.

XVII

THEY'D KEPT THE corpse on ice, in cold storage and out of the public eye, for almost two full weeks. Now, with six civilians dead and the city's population frightened and outraged, a top-level political decision was made to ease the pressure by putting the body on display, parading it about for everyone to see.

A Staff Sergeant, six foot two and resplendent in his dress uniform, brought a silver bugle to his lips and began to play. On cue, the eight pall-bearers slowly lowered the mortal remains of Detective David Ulysses Atkinson into his grave.

Mrs Atkinson, a thin, bony woman with a wide mouth and her son's dark and passionate eyes, began to cry quietly. Inspector Bradley quickly offered her his handkerchief. It was Irish linen, brand new, precisely folded and rigid with starch. Mrs Atkinson dabbed at her brimming eyes and then enveloped her button nose in the handkerchief and blew long and loud.

Behind them, at the base of the grassy, gently sloping hill that led to the graveyard's parking lot, stood a sparse and restless crowd — the usual mix of good friends and bad of the bereaved family, passers-by, the idly curious, death junkies.

On the flat ground surrounding the gravesite more than seven hundred uniformed city police had gathered, and there were also contingents of scarlet-clad Mounties from the neighbouring communities of Burnaby, North Vancouver, Richmond and Surrey, as well as municipal cops from West Vancouver, Squamish, and New Westminster.

The brass and the politicians, thought Bradley, were getting exactly what they wanted: a public relations gesture in the form of a visible and highly photogenic testimonial to a good cop who had been shot down in the line of duty, while in hot pursuit of the .460 Magnum killer. It was bad luck that just as the last mournful notes spilled from the bugle, the thin drizzle that had been leaking out of the sky all day long abruptly turned into a heavy downpour, a drenching onslaught that caused the sombre and orderly ranks of policemen to break up, fall apart like wet cardboard as the coppers hustled to keep themselves and their powder dry.

Bradley watched with a mixture of amusement and dismay as hundreds of gaudy and entirely inappropriate umbrellas blossomed, lending the funeral a bright and festive air. The probability and consequences of inclement weather had been discussed at length at one of the tactics meetings held earlier in the week. It had been suggested that the department purchase a thousand identical black umbrellas, but because of the prohibitive expense the idea had been reluctantly discarded. A complete ban on umbrellas had also been kicked around, until someone had pointed out that among the rank-and-file, the common cold was already quite common enough.

Over by the grave, a gust of wind rattled the protective plastic wrapping on a hand-held television camera, distracting Bradley's attention. He watched as the cameraman moved in for a closeup of the Mayor, who was standing perilously near the edge of the grave, struggling to dump a shovelful of wet, gluey earth on to the coffin.

Behind the Mayor, Superintendent Ford stood solemnly, his expression resourceful and determined, his hands at his sides. Only the nervous twitching of his thumbs betrayed the tension he felt as he waited for his stint under the television lights, the sharp and penetrating questions of the network reporters.

Bradley's attention was deflected again as the Honour Guard stepped forward to raise their rifles and fire the first of three crisp volleys. He moved aside as the priest shuffled over and laid a soft white hand on Mrs Atkinson's shoulder. The second and then the third volleys were fired into the leaden clouds. The sound of the shots echoed off the slope behind them, drowning the priest's words of comfort. Bradley found himself squinting into the lens of a camera, but it was the bereaved mother they were interested in, not him. A moment later the crowd began to break up. The priest seemed to have taken Mrs Atkinson in hand. Bradley took advantage of the situation to slip away, abandoning his ruined handkerchief.

Willows and Parker had kept busy discreetly taking photographs of the civilians at the funeral. Now, as the last of the shots were fired, Willows tucked the camera under his arm and they began the uphill climb towards the parking lot.

Partway up the slope, George Franklin and Farley Spears stood waiting for them. There was a brief jostling of umbrellas as Franklin fell in next to Parker. There was no room for him to walk abreast of her on the narrow path, and his shoes darkened as he strode through the lush, rain-soaked grass. "We finally ran down the last of the suspects on the short list you gave Bradley," he said to Parker. "The guy's name was Collins, remember?"

"Jerry Collins," said Parker.

"Yeah, well, he's been dead for the past six months. Rolled his car on a patch of black ice on the highway outside of Prince George last November, on his way home from a bar."

"There's no question that he was positively identified?"

"No question," said Franklin.

"Some people will do damn near anything to duck a murder rap," said Spears. He grinned at Parker and she looked at him as if he was a bug. The grin faded.

"George?" said Willows.

"Yeah, what?"

"I noticed you spent some time with Atkinson's mother. How's she taking it?"

Franklin shrugged. "Not too bad, I guess. I said hello because I figured I owed her one last chance to cuff me around a little, let off some steam. But she's stopped blaming me. All she wanted to talk about was how much she liked my tie."

"I noticed it myself," said Parker. "It looks good on you. What is it, silk?"

"Rayon, probably," said Franklin. "My wife buys my ties. I never owned a silk one in my life."

"Well whatever it is, it looks terrific," said Parker firmly.

But the truth was, Franklin looked awful. His scuffed brown shoes and Argyle socks and the cuffs of his pants were soaked through, but he felt so bad he hardly noticed. He'd lost a lot of his excess weight since the murder of Atkinson: almost twenty pounds in less than two weeks. The weight loss had been far too

143

rapid, leaving him feeling listless and weak. And he was smoking more now than ever before, in a futile attempt to ease his nervous tension, the ever-growing burden of his guilt. The short walk up the hill had exhausted him, and the funeral had left him emotionally drained, empty. He was breathing through his mouth but he couldn't seem to get enough air, his heart was pounding furiously in his chest. When he coughed it sounded as if his lungs were full of rust.

The path levelled out as they reached the top of the hill. Twenty yards away a high wrought-iron gate set in a trim boxwood hedge provided access to the parking lot. By the time they reached the gate, Franklin seemed to have recovered both his spirits and his wind. His position as assistant liaison officer put him right in the middle of the information web, and he had a tidbit of news for Willows that was hot off the presses. As they passed under the dripping iron gate and into the parking lot, he said, "Did you know that the crime lab finally tracked down the missing container of coleslaw, Jack?"

"Where was it?"

"Tucked away in the back of that old fridge they've got in the lounge. A clerk named Jane Patrick thought it was part of somebody's lunch. We know it was her because Goldstein found her prints all over the lid. She'd pried it off to take a look inside, see what was in there."

"Were her prints the only ones on the container?" said Parker.

"No, but they were the only clean ones. Goldstein did lift a few partials, though, and most of a thumb. Enough for a positive identification, but not to run through the computer or take into court." Franklin paused, and then added, "Goldstein figures the prints belong to a woman."

"Why is that?" said Willows.

"Because they were so small," said Franklin. He looked down at his own large, ungainly hands, the spatulate, nicotine-stained fingers. The hands were ugly. He stuffed them away in the pockets of his raincoat.

They had come to Parker's Volkswagen. Franklin said goodbye and he and Spears walked away, their feet crunching on the gravel. Parker fumbled in her purse for her keys. She unlocked the car and got inside, rolled her window down a couple of inches and slammed the door, rolled the window back up. Willows waited for her to reach across to unlock his door, then climbed in beside her. He leaned back in the bucket-seat and closed his eyes. Parker put the key in the ignition and started the engine. It chugged and hummed noisily. She switched on the windshield wipers, clearing the glass. Through a ragged gap in the hedge she watched a bright orange machine creep up to the loose mound of earth beside the open grave.

"You know something?" said Willows, opening his eyes.

"What?"

"Every time somebody gets shot, we find something at the crime scene that the killer has left behind. Spent brass, an ashtray full of cigarette butts, a pair of earmuffs, coleslaw."

"Nothing was left behind when Atkinson was shot," Parker pointed out.

"That was a different situation. For some reason the killer was prowling around in Phasia Palinkas' apartment when Franklin and Atkinson showed up. Atkinson surprised him and got shot. But the killing wasn't planned, it wasn't worked out in advance. And Atkinson wasn't a member of the singles club."

"Okay," said Parker. "What's your point?"

"The point is that we've been wasting a hell of a lot of time chasing all this stuff down. Trying to make the pieces of physical evidence fit into a puzzle that doesn't even exist. Take the shoe that was left in the road after the cabbie was shot, the shoe with the heart stitched over the arch."

"The same shoe we found in the picture in Flora McCormick's office," said Parker.

"Wrong," said Willows. "It looks like the same shoe, but it isn't. I had Mel Dutton enlarge the picture. The shoe in the road was brand new, the one in the photograph shows plenty of wear. Also, Dutton figures the one in the picture was several sizes smaller."

"What are you saying, that the picture was a plant, that the two shoes don't have anything to do with each other?"

"Something along those lines."

Parker thought about it for a moment and then said, "You think the killer's been toying with us, playing a game."

145

"That's what it looks like to me."

"I don't know," said Parker. "There has to be more to it than that."

Parker leaned forward and used the back of her hand to wipe condensation from the windshield. Down on the flat, the operator of the orange machine was manipulating an articulated metal arm with a metal bucket on the end. The arm suddenly jerked sideways. A fountain of earth sprayed up into the air and tumbled into the grave. In the same moment, a puff of oily blue smoke spouted from the machine's exhaust pipe. The arm swung back for another strike at the mound of earth. The blue smoke was pounded to shreds by the rain.

Parker released the emergency brake, put the car in reverse and backed up in a sweeping arc, turning to face the exit of the parking lot. She changed into first and let out the clutch. Gravel crunched under the wheels with the fragile sound of breaking shells.

The wiper blade on Willows' side was frayed and needed replacing. The worn rubber flopped wearily back and forth, smearing the rain across the glass, blurring his field of vision and leaving him feeling mildly claustrophobic. Willows turned away from the windshield and looked at Parker, studying her profile, admiring the firm, graceful lines of neck and jaw, the tilt of her nose, the sloping planes of her cheek and the soft curve of her lips, the light in her eyes. It had been a mistake, spending the night with her. The time she'd spent in the morgue had frightened and depressed her, and he'd taken full advantage of her despair. Not to mention that he was still a married man, even if he no longer had a wife.

At the far end of the Property Room at 312 Main there is a large steel vault that is used for the short-term emergency storage of small, high-value items such as jewellery, cash and hard drugs. To the right of the safe there is a bicycle rack that is occupied at any given time by half a dozen or more expensive English and Italian bicycles. But almost all of the floor space in the property room is filled with row after row of unpainted plywood shelves. The shelves sag with the weight of stolen television sets, stereo

146

components, sporting goods, typewriters and computers, automobile parts, musical instruments — almost anything of value that a determined thief or thieves could carry through an open door or window to a waiting car or truck.

The only access to the room is through a steel mesh door. For longer than anyone can remember, the door has been guarded by a horse. The horse is a chestnut, a stallion. The stallion stands seventeen hands high, but his lustrous brown eyes are made of German glass, and his flared nostrils are layered with a fine grey dust. In the crowded, low-ceilinged room, the horse seems larger than life. But moths have been at him, and pranksters, too. In order to read the number on his identification tag, it is necessary to crouch at the rear of the animal, lift its tail, and look up.

Years ago, someone had stuck a stolen bowler hat on the beast's head, wedged a cheap cigar in its mouth, and called it Whinnie. The hat had disappeared on a rainy day and an unidentified thief had eventually smoked the cigar, but the name had stuck like glue.

Whinnie's head cast a wedge-shaped shadow across a double pedestal oak desk (also tagged) that stood in the corner on the far side of the doorway. Jack Willows sat wearily at the desk, shoulders hunched, staring sightlessly down at the mass of physical evidence collected from the four murder sites. It was two o'clock in the morning. Willows' skin was pale and crumpled. There were dark circles under his eyes. He needed a bath, and a change of clothes, and a shave.

When Corporal Bernie Watts pushed his way through the door carrying two thick white mugs of steaming coffee, Willows didn't bother to look up. Watts was the duty officer. He came into the room like a man on a tightrope, moving slowly and cautiously, holding the mugs of hot coffee well away from his body. Despite his caution there was a certain amount of spillage as he pivoted towards the desk, and he was forced to perform an impromptu little jig to save the mirror polish on his shoes.

"Damn it," Watts said, "those last couple of steps are always the hardest, aren't they?"

Willows considered the question for a moment, and then said, "What?"

Watts shook his head and rolled his eyes. "Have some coffee, Jack."

Willows accepted the proffered mug, sipped gingerly, winced.

"Too strong, is it?" said Watts.

"If you have to ask, Bernie, your taste buds are in real serious trouble."

Chuckling, Watts knelt and unlocked the bottom right-hand drawer of the desk, pulled the drawer all the way out. He had a bottle of Lambs Navy Rum tucked away at the back of the drawer, hidden behind a stack of old *Playboy* and *Penthouse* magazines. There was about an inch and a half of liquor in the bottle. Watts poured it equally into the two mugs, stirred it in with his Bic pen.

Willows held up his mug. "Thanks, Bernie. Mud."

The rum had given the coffee an extra dimension of warmth. Willows felt a slow trickle of energy seeping back into his body. He sat back in his chair, put his feet up on the desk.

Watts pulled cigarettes and matches from the breast pocket of his starched blue shirt. He lit up and tossed the spent and smoking match halfway across the desk, into an ashtray made out of an automobile piston. Waving the cigarette at the evidence bags scattered across the surface of the desk, he said, "Real weird case, eh Jack?"

"Looks that way," said Willows tersely.

It was clear from Willows' tone of voice that the subject wasn't open to discussion. Watts frowned. Nobody but nobody ever told him what was going on upstairs. All he ever heard was faint whisperings, uncertain rumours. Frustrated, he flicked half an inch of ash into the piston, and decided to attack Willows from another angle. What he'd do was ramble on about nothing in particular until Willows had to say something back, speak up in self-defence, even if it was only to shut him up. Once he got Willows talking, he'd gradually work the conversation around to the string of unsolved shootings, find out if the papers were right about the homicide cops not knowing what the hell was going on, or if homicide was all over the case and getting set to make a bust.

"Speaking of coffee," Watts said to Willows, "do you by any chance remember a guy named Phil Taylor?"

"Skinny face, jug ears?"

"Yeah, that's him. Well, whenever Phil wanted a coffee, he'd take a hike all the way up to the third floor and steal a cup from that machine they got in vice. Said vice had a special blend you couldn't find anywhere else in the building."

"No kidding," said Willows. Because he was drinking Watts' rum, he felt a minimal obligation to hold up his end of the conversation.

"Even then," said Watts, "he wasn't all that happy with the situation. I told him, hey, if you don't like anybody else's brew, why not bring an electric kettle down here and make your own? Charge fifty cents a cup and get rich, retire early. You know what he said? That he was a cop, not a fucking caterer." Watts flicked another length of ash into the piston. "It must've been a year at least before I found out all those trips upstairs every day had nothing at all to do with coffee."

"Oh yeah?" said Willows.

"Turns out he was dating one of the clerks up there on the third floor. Or he'd been going out with her and they'd broke up and he couldn't handle it. Or maybe it was just that he was hot for her and kept asking her to go out with him but she wasn't interested. I dunno. Point is, and this is what I've been getting at, the coffee's equally bad all over the building, upstairs and down. Doesn't matter where you work, more than a couple of cups a day, you're asking for trouble."

Willows lifted his feet off the desk and leaned forward in his chair, was swallowed by the shadow of the dead horse. "Here's to democracy, Bernie. Equally bad coffee for one and all."

"I'll drink to just about anything," said Watts, raising his mug, "but to tell the truth I tend to favour the Police State. And not just because I've got an inside track, either. I've thought about it a lot, Jack, and the way I see it, the main problem with society is a lack of organization. People have too many choices, too much to choose from. Doesn't matter whether we're talking about haircuts or microwave ovens. Too much choice breeds nothing but confusion and discontent. Like Phil Taylor, wasting his time running around trying to find the perfect cup of coffee. You want to know what my motto is? Give Fascism a chance."

Watts winked broadly to let Willows know that he wasn't a nut, that he was at least partly kidding. He took a long last drag on his cigarette, and leaned across the desk to squash out the butt in the ashtray.

Willows suddenly came alive. Jerking forward in the chair, he grabbed Watts' wrist and snatched the cigarette out of his hand. Watts stared at Willows as Willows pinched the cigarette in two pieces, and dropped the burning coal in the ashtray.

"Hey," said Watts, finally reacting, "what d'you think you're doing?"

Willows stripped the thick paper wrapping from the filter and tore the filter in half lengthways. He held the shredded material up to the light, turning it slowly on the pedestal of his fingers, examining it from every angle.

"Smoke much, Bernie?"

Watts shook his head. "I wouldn't say so. Pack and a half a day, maybe. Why d'you ask?"

"You always smoke filter tips?"

"No, I switched over a couple of years ago."

"Why?"

Watts shrugged. "The usual reasons. Cut down on the tar and nicotine, all that gunk. Get the wife and kids off my back. Live for ever." He drained his mug. "Why all the questions, Jack?"

"The filters really work, do they?"

"Yeah, they work."

"Watch," said Willows. He opened one of the plastic evidence bags with an uncharacteristic flourish, and shook out several lipstick-stained cigarette butts. "These were found in the ashtray of the car used in the murder of the second victim," he said.

"Phasia Palinkas, right? The Greek woman. And the car was a silver Mercedes."

Willows smiled. "Been following the case, Bernie?"

"In the papers," said Watts diffidently. "Off and on."

Willows picked up one of the butts that had spilled from the evidence bag. He used his thumbnail to split the filter in half and put the two halves down on the desk next to the filter from Watts' cigarette. Watts watched carefully, as if Willows was an accomplished magician who might inadvertently let slip a trick or two.

Willows nudged the torn filters across the desk towards him. "Notice any difference between the filter from your cigarette and the one from the Mercedes?"

"Sure," said Watts, nodding. He picked up the filter from the car. "Mine is stained with nicotine, this one's pure as the driven snow."

"How do you explain that?"

"Could only be one reason, Jack. Whoever lit this one let it burn down without actually smoking it. So no smoke was drawn through the filter, you see what I mean?"

Willows tapped the evidence bag. "They're all like that," he said. "The whole bag full."

"What that means," said Bernie, "is that the killer lit almost a whole pack of cigarettes but didn't smoke a single one of them." Comically, he scratched his head. "I don't get it. What's the point?"

Willows glanced at his watch. It was quarter past two. The government liquor stores were all closed and the nearest bootlegger that he knew about was more than five miles away. Smiling, he said, "Why don't you haul out that spare bottle of yours, Bernie. We'll talk it over, see if we can come up with something."

"Yeah, sure," said Watts. "Break the case wide open." But his voice betrayed his excitement, and he was already groping in his pants pocket for the key to the bottom left-hand drawer of his desk.

XVIII

MIRIAM OKAHASHI REMOVED her designer prescription glasses and gently massaged the bridge of her nose where the stylish oversized plastic frames had left painful little dents in her flesh. She sighed imperceptibly as she put the glasses back on, stole a peek at her brand new Piaget.

It was 4:54 p.m. There were six more minutes remaining in the session, only six more minutes left in the week. Miriam had spent much of the session silently counting off the seconds, but there was only the faintest hint of impatience in her almond eyes as she glanced across the broad expanse of beige carpet at Raymond Cooley. Cooley was sitting hunched on the edge of the black leather Chesterfield, staring sightlessly down at the carpet with his elbows resting on his bony knees. His dirty blond hair, which he liked to comb straight back from his narrow skull David Bowie style, hung down in front of his sallow face like a frayed curtain.

Miriam listened to the sound of the rush-hour traffic floating in through her open window, the translucent green curtains. Perversely, she wished that she was out there, part of the jam. This was her fifth session with Cooley, and it was turning out to be even more of a waste of time than the first four hours had been.

As always, Cooley was wearing his dark blue suit, the white shirt with the ink-stained breast pocket, a pair of black slip-ons, no tie. He habitually sat in absolute silence, perfectly motionless, for as long as fifteen minutes at a time. Miriam had quickly learned that any attempt on her part to encourage Cooley to speak before he was ready would only result in a lengthier silence.

When he finally did decide to talk to her, he often strung his words together so rapidly and with so little concern for subject matter or syntax that she had difficulty understanding him, following his train of thought. But if she interjected, no matter how delicately, to ask him to repeat a word or a phrase, he invariably retreated into himself, became surly and uncommunicative. Even when he was allowed to speak without interruption, he always stopped talking as abruptly as he'd begun, often in mid-sentence or even in the middle of a word. Then, nervously pressing back the soft flesh of his cuticles with the edge of his thumbnail, he'd resume staring blindly down at the carpet. Miriam found it all rather boring. She took another peek at the Piaget. One minute down and five to go.

Cooley's eyes appeared to be closed, but he was covertly watching Miriam through his curtain of hair. She was a real dish, no doubt about it. He loved those big brown eyes, her small, pouty mouth, the glossy black hair. She had a nice body, too. Slim, but with curves in all the right places. He thought about what it was going to be like when he finally decided to make his move, the move he knew she'd been waiting for ever since he'd first walked into her office. What he'd do was keep it simple. Stand up right in the middle of one of his silences, take her by surprise. Women liked to be surprised. He'd maybe flick a bit of lint off his sleeve, and then stroll casually over to her desk. He'd hold out his hand as he stepped towards her, and she'd come gracefully to her feet, reaching out to him. He would gently kiss the palm of her hand and then suddenly thrust the tip of his tongue between her fingers, shocking and arousing her, giving her just a taste of what he had planned for her.

He imagined her gasp of pleasure, the look of yearning in her dark, liquid eyes. Somehow they would end up on the black leather couch. As he began to take off her clothes he kissed her tenderly on the throat, murmured endless reassurances.

Her bra was lacy and insubstantial, just like the ones they wore in the magazines. The clasp fell apart at his touch. He threw the bra over his shoulder and kissed her high, firm breasts, watched the nipples rise like mushrooms. He pushed her skirt up around her waist as she wriggled and squirmed beneath him. Her panties were black silk, provocatively cut. He raised an enquiring eyebrow, teasing her, and she blushed, her smooth skin

153

darkening. He slid the panties down around her ankles and then crushed them against his mouth. As he inhaled the musky fragrance of her perfume, his need for her became overpowering. He sat up and began to undress, forcing himself not to rush, to take his time. Miriam couldn't wait. She had completely lost control. She reached blindly towards him, shamelessly tearing at his clothes. . . .

Sweat stung Cooley's eyes. He wiped his face with the back of his hand, blinking rapidly. Miriam was admiring her new watch again. He took his comb out of the breast pocket of his suit, ran it vigorously through his listless hair.

Miriam was watching him. Now that he had her attention, he began to speak.

"I was thinking on the way over that this is our fifth session together and that we . . ." He frowned, running out of juice. He had lost, as he feared he would, the thread of his intent. He looked down, staring into the depths of the carpet, and then looked quickly up. Miriam was paying strict attention to him, doing her best to help him along. He ran the comb across the back of his hand. Each tooth left a fading white line across his skin. He pressed harder, making the skin turn red.

This week the comb was white. Last week it had been yellow. The week before last, blue. Miriam idly wondered if the changing colours were of any significance, or if Cooley was simply the kind of man who kept losing things.

As if sensing her thoughts, Cooley slipped the comb back into his pocket. He was ready to start talking again.

"After all the time we've been together, wouldn't you agree that we're getting to know each other pretty well?"

"I'm glad you feel that way," said Miriam. She mustered a smile. "Was there something in particular you wanted to talk about today, something you'd like to discuss now that we've spent some time together?"

Cooley shrugged, the heavily padded shoulders of his suit jacket rising and falling comically. "I've been losing a lot of friends lately. Not that I had all that many to begin with. It seems to me that I should try to make some new friends, replacements. Out with the old and in with the new. But it's hard to meet people. If you walk right up to them, they become frightened. So would you mind telling me what the hell I'm supposed to do? Is there a secret, some kind of trick I don't know about?"

"Why have you been losing friends?" said Miriam.

"It's your fault," said Cooley. "You told me I'd feel better about myself if I was more assertive. So I've been making a real serious effort not to let people walk all over me. For example that time at the zoo. But half the time I get so worked up and things get out of hand or I wait until it's too late. Time passes too fast. The guy is way down at the other end of the block and I'm still figuring out what to say to him. Or I go overboard and get physical." Cooley took out his comb. The comb had a handle about four inches long, that tapered gradually to a needle-sharp point. "I stuck it in a pencil-sharpener," Cooley said. "Maybe one of these days I'm going to stick it into some wise guy who makes a smart remark."

The intercom buzzed, harsh, persistent, very loud. It was Miriam's secretary, alerting her to the fact that it was five o'clock and that the last session of the day was over, that it was time to go home. Miriam reached across her desk to turn the buzzer off. She looked openly at the Piaget. The small but perfectly cut diamond set in the crown of the watch was reflected in the polished mahogany of the desktop. It reminded her, as it was intended to, of her latest lover, Norbert. Norbert was a pro football player, a tackle for the BC Lions. Miriam had met him a little over a month ago, at a party in Caulfield Cove given by one of the team's directors. Even in the crowd of jocks, Norbert had stood out. He was six foot four, weighed two hundred and thirty pounds, and was as hard and black as a lump of anthracite. Miriam had initially been attracted by the sheer size and bulk of him, but as the evening progressed and she slowly learned to decipher his Mississippi accent, she discovered that there was a pretty good brain lurking under his unruly Afro. So they could talk, too, when they were in the mood.

Miriam leaned forward in her chair, resting her elbows on the desk and making a tent of her fingers. "I think you should get rid of that comb," she said quietly but firmly. "If the police happened to find it on you, they could lay a charge."

155

"Like what?"

"Carrying a concealed weapon."

Miriam tried to make eye contact, but Cooley kept his head down. He glared at the carpet, his eyes hot and wet. "What if I told you that sometimes I get so mad I'm afraid I'm going to lose control, go completely crazy!"

Miriam smiled sympathetically. "This may come as a surprise to you, but every once in a while I feel that way myself."

"You do?" said Cooley, incredulous.

"Yes, of course." And right now is one of those times, thought Miriam. According to the Piaget, it was now two minutes past five, and she was running on a very tight schedule. Her thoughts drifted to the evening that lay ahead. She and Norbert had planned an early dinner, and left the rest of the night free. Which meant, she fervently hoped, that they were going to spend the time pounding the stuffing out of Norbert's kingsize Sealy Posturpedic.

Miriam jerked upright and almost cried out loud as something warm and moist fell across her wrist. It was Cooley's hand. His face was so close to hers that she could smell his breath, sour and defeated. "Shall I make another appointment with Sheila on my way out?" he said.

Miriam nodded, unwilling to trust her voice.

Cooley reluctantly let go of her wrist, turned his back on her and strode out of the office. Miriam looked at the Piaget. Five minutes past five. The crystal was wet with Cooley's sweat, and the gold numerals beneath the thin film of salty liquid seemed distorted, as if they had been warped by the heat of his sad embrace.

The building directly across the street from Miriam Okahashi's office was three storeys high and faced with red brick. The building was in the midst of extensive renovations, and it was vacant. The sniper weaved his way through the clutter of construction materials, took the steps up to the top floor two and three at a time. He was wearing a new pair of shoes, and the high heels clattered on the naked concrete as he climbed.

There was a small landing with a steel rail around it at the top of the stairs, a hatch that had been built to provide access to the roof. The sniper paused to catch his breath, then unbolted the door and pushed it open. Except for half a dozen looping high-voltage lines, the view across the flat tar-and-gravel roof was completely unobstructed. Crouching, he snapped open the rifle case and removed the Winchester. Peering through the scope, he was able to detect a vague movement through the pale green curtains. He checked his watch. It was three minutes to five. He lowered the rifle and drew back the bolt, jacked a round into the chamber.

Nothing to do now but wait. He only had a few minutes to go, but he knew from past experience that a few minutes could be a very long time. He thought about lighting a cigarette, decided against it. Miriam Okahashi's window was wide open, even though it had been raining steadily all day long. She had to be a fresh-air fiend. Or maybe she had a problem with the fruitcakes' smoking. A pigeon flew across the sniper's field of vision, and settled on one of the high-tension wires. He lifted the rifle and took a bead on the bird's ridiculously puffed-out chest. It blinked at him with little yellow eyes, and edged nervously sideways along the wire. The sniper's cheek itched fiercely. He scratched himself and then stared in mute surprise at the smear of bright pink makeup on the blunt fingers of his glove. Cursing, he tore off the glove and flung it across the roof. He was going to have to remember to buy a few more pairs, his supply was running low. The cost of keeping up appearances, the high price of success! The sniper chuckled, his mood changing. There was a movement in the office. The curtains shifted as if from a slight gust of wind. The sniper raised the rifle, pressed his cheek against the stock.

Miriam shrugged into her bright yellow Baert raincoat and picked up her purse and her umbrella. She was halfway to the door when she remembered the open window. Her heels, as she hurriedly retraced her steps, left an almost perfectly straight line of dimples in the beige rug.

The window opened outwards on a complex double-hinge mechanism. Miriam brushed aside the curtain and pulled on the handle. The window glided smoothly shut. She fastened the lock and let the curtain fall softly back, turned to leave.

The curtain ballooned towards her as if someone standing behind it had suddenly thrust out his arm, reaching towards her. In the same instant there was the sound of a shot, and the impact of the bullet slamming into her throat, cutting off her scream, slicing through both carotid arteries and her spine. She staggered backwards, her head lolling, chin on chest. Her hip struck a corner of the desk and she spun sideways, dead on her feet, then fell across the black leather couch and slid on a river of blood, face down on to the carpet.

Inspector Homer Bradley stood at his window with his hands in his pockets, staring morosely down through the slanting rain at the adjoining construction site. The foundation of the new building had been laid a week ago, and now men in black rain slickers were removing the plywood forms and exposing the raw, green-tinged cement beneath. Soon the framework of steel I-beams would come spouting up towards him, plunging his office into eternal shadow, stripping him of his view. He lifted his eyes, and looked out across the dark and gloomy harbour.

A Russian freighter pushed against the wind and outgoing tide towards the grainery next to the Second Narrows bridge, the bow wave out of all proportion to the vessel's slow progress through the water. High above the ship a dozen or more herring gulls flew on a direct line towards the rocky, protein-rich shores of Third Beach. As Bradley watched, the hindmost gull suddenly peeled away from the formation, spiralling swiftly down until it was lost among the confusion of the waves.

Bradley went over to his desk, sat down, helped himself to a cigar from his carved cedar box.

The telephone rang. The ringing seemed unnaturally loud, as if the instrument was somehow trying to transmit the urgency of the caller. Bradley struck a match on the underside of his desk, got the cigar going to his satisfaction, and picked up the receiver.

The call was from a motorcycle cop named Layton. He had radioed in from his Harley and been patched in to Bradley's office through the emergency switchboard. Bradley's ear was filled with the hiss and gurgle of traffic, the erratic throbbing of the Harley's 1200 c.c. engine. He blew smoke at the ceiling. Layton made a big deal of identifying himself. His voice was fragmented, muddy. No doubt it was the quality of the telephone connection but Bradley couldn't help picturing Layton's front teeth, the gaps filled with large, furry insects, the fauna of the open road. He had to ask Layton to repeat himself three times before he finally understood that a psychiatrist named Miriam Okahashi had been nearly decapitated by a single shot fired from a large-calibre rifle.

When he hung up the telephone he was standing, and he happened to be facing the window. The rain was coming down much harder now, a torrent of fat drops that rushed vertically towards the earth. The Russian freighter had passed out of his line of vision. The punishing rain had emptied the sky of birds.

Miriam Okahashi's posture as she lay face down on the beige carpet suggested that she was still trying to run from the bullet that had struck her down. Her right leg was bent sharply, as if in mid-stride, and her left arm was flung forward. Her glossy black hair was in disarray, and a few shards of glass sparkled in the pool of blood that surrounded her head like a dark and monstrous halo. Layton, pointing out the location of the bullet hole, actually put his finger in it. Bradley stared at him, and he blushed, and turned away. Bradley was staring out the window at the red brick building across the street when Parker, George Franklin, Farley Spears, Jerry Goldstein, Mel Dutton and several other homicide cops filed into the office. Bradley assumed they had all come up in the same crowded elevator. He crooked his finger at Parker and Franklin, stepped over the body and pushed his way through to the door. The three of them took the elevator back down to the lobby and Bradley led them out of the building and into the rain.

The street was crowded with police vehicles that had monitored Layton's call and scooted towards the crime scene on the off-chance of picking up a piece of the action. Civilian traffic was backing up fast. Bradley, followed by Parker and Franklin, threaded his way through six lanes of stalled traffic and across the sidewalk to the glass front doors of the red brick building. The left-side door was slightly ajar and Bradley saw that it was being held open by a spent .460 Magnum cartridge. The cartridge dropped tinkling to the floor when he yanked open the door.

Franklin stooped and tried to insert the point of his pen into the shell to pick it up. But the mouth of the casing had been flattened into an oval by the pressure of the door, and the pen would not fit into it. Bradley saw that Franklin had a problem. There was a bent nail on the floor. He kicked it over. Franklin used the nail to pick up the casing. He dropped the casing into a small glassine evidence bag and put the bag in his pocket.

The sniper's high-heeled shoes had left a clear trail, both coming and going, on the dusty concrete floor. They followed the footsteps through the débris of construction, up the three flights of stairs and through the access hatch to the roof. Just to the left of the doorway stood an open bottle of Beefeater gin, two miniature Schweppes tonic bottles and a tall glass on a soggy cardboard container.

"Get Goldstein up here on the double," Bradley said to Parker.

Parker turned and went back down the stairs as fast as she could go.

Franklin lit a cigarette. Down on the street a horn blared and someone shouted an oath. Franklin blew out his match, rubbed it between his thumb and index finger, dropped it into the cuff of his pants. Behind him, Willows stepped out on the roof, gravel crunching under his heels, his collar turned up against the rain.

"Where the hell have you been?" said Bradley.

"Excavating," said Willows. He handed Bradley the battered 500 grain copper-jacketed bullet that had ripped through Miriam Okahashi's throat.

"Where'd you find it?"

"Buried in a 1913 German-language edition of Jung's *Critique of Psychoanalysis*."

"Of course," said Bradley. "When you think about it, where else could it be."

Franklin flicked cigarette ash into his pocket.

Willows looked around the roof, saw the Beefeater and Schweppes bottles, the empty glass drinking up the rain.

"What's it look like to you?" said Bradley.

"As if he sat in the doorway out of the rain and had himself a couple of drinks while he waited for a clear shot."

160

"The dirty bastard," said Bradley, nodding his agreement. He turned as Parker, Goldstein and Mel Dutton stepped out on to the roof. Goldstein waved his arm and a black umbrella appeared as if by magic above his curly blond head. He offered the umbrella to Parker but she refused to accept it. Bradley kicked at the roof, and sent a dozen small round pebbles skittering over the edge. "Why," he said to no one in particular, "would a woman like Miriam Okahashi join a fucking singles club?"

"She was working on her thesis," said Willows. "It was part of her research."

Bradley stared malevolently at him, rain dripping steadily from his nose. "How did you find that out?"

"Norbert told me."

"Who in hell is Norbert?"

"Norbert Waterman. He plays tackle for the Lions. He's also Miriam Okahashi's boyfriend. They had an early dinner date and he dropped by hoping to catch her before she left for home. Found her dead on the floor and ran out into the street, right into Brooks Layton."

"Who?"

"The motorcycle cop."

"Right," said Bradley.

"Scared the shit out of Layton, the way I heard it," said Jerry Goldstein. He grinned at Willows, but Willows' mind was occupied with George Franklin, who was standing motionless in the rain like a prop waiting to be used. A wet cigarette dangled from Franklin's mouth. His skin was slack, and his face had an unhealthy greyish tinge. His dark eyes, sunken and haggard, stared unseeingly into the middle distance, the haze of rain. His movements, when he flicked the dead cigarette in a high arc that carried it down into the street, were strangely mechanical, almost lifeless. The shooting in the Palinkas apartment, Willows thought, had resulted in one instant murder and a second that was ongoing. He wondered what would happen when they eventually caught the sniper. Would his capture or death prove to be George Franklin's salvation?

Behind Willows, Mel Dutton crouched and took a half-step

backwards as he focused on the two Schweppes bottles and the empty glass. Something slippery and soft gave beneath the heel of his shoe. He looked down and saw that he had stepped on a slice of lime.

XIX

WILLOWS WAVED HIS arm and made an exaggerated pouring
motion. Freddy got a glass from the rack, dropped in a couple of
ice cubes and added an ounce and a half of Cutty. He was pouring
Willows' third drink in less than an hour, and he wasn't very
happy about it, because in his considerable experience customers
who drank too much were just as big a pain in the ass as
customers who didn't drink at all. He picked up the glass of
Scotch and carried it over to Willows, put it down on the table in
front of him.

Willows didn't look up. Freddy smiled down at him and said,
"Take it easy, Jack. All this running back and forth is putting a
real strain on my pacemaker."

"Where's Sally," said Willows, "doesn't she usually work
Monday nights?"

"Sally's in bed. You know who with?"

Willows sipped at his drink. Finally, he looked up.

"The 'flu," said Freddy.

"Next time," said Willows, "bring me a double and save
yourself a trip."

Freddy had to get the last word in. "You're all something," he
said, "but it ain't heart."

Three-quarters of an hour and two rounds later, Claire Parker
hurried into the bar. Parker was wearing a burgundy parka,
faded jeans, bright yellow gumboots. Her face was flushed with
excitement, wet with rain. She gave Freddy his biggest smile of
the week, and ordered a draft beer. Freddy nodded, and pointed
at the booth where Willows was sitting.

Parker's coat left a smear of damp on the dark brown
naugahyde as she slipped into the seat opposite Willows. He gave
her a quizzical look.

"Hi there," said Parker. "Care to buy a lady a drink?"

"I thought ladies bought their own drinks, if they drank at all."

"Better wind your watch, Jack. It's running about twenty years late."

Willows helped himself to a mouthful of Scotch, put his glass back down on the formica hard enough to make the ice jump.

"Are you drunk?" said Parker.

"Not yet, but I'm working on it."

"That's the main thing, not to stop working."

"Yeah, right." Willows was very much aware of the delicate odour of Parker's perfume, the faint smile hovering in the corners of her mouth. He regarded her carefully, wondering what the hell she was up to.

Freddy arrived with Parker's beer, and Parker said, "Where's Sally?"

"Sick," said Freddy shortly. He'd guessed that Willows in his sour mood had already told Parker about his little joke and that she expected him to try it out on her, that it was a setup.

"What's wrong with her?" said Parker.

"Stomach 'flu. She had me up all night, running back and forth with ginger ale, blankets, hot-water bottles."

"Words of wisdom," said Willows.

Freddy forced a smile.

"I hope she gets better soon," said Parker.

"Thanks," said Freddy. He gave the table a quick wipe, and drifted back to the bar.

Parker waited until he had gone and then lifted her glass and said, "Here's looking at me, kid."

"What'd you do, guide a boy scout across the street?"

"Even better," said Parker. She'd stopped kidding around; she sounded almost as sober as she looked.

"Tell me about it."

"I'd rather show you," said Parker. "Drink up, and let's hit the road."

Twenty minutes later, Parker unlocked the door to Miriam Okahashi's outer office, and reached inside to switch on the lights. The reception area had the same beige carpet as the inner office. It was full of light oak furniture, glossy magazines, and the

164

kind of plants that thrived on fluorescent light. Muzak seeped from speakers concealed in the acoustical tile ceiling. Parker used another key to get them into the psychiatrist's office, and Willows' curiosity finally got the better of him.

"Where'd you get the keys?"

"From Norbert. She always kept a spare set in his apartment." Avoiding the blood and chalked outline on the carpet, Parker crossed to the bullet-punctured window and opened it wide. "Come here, take a look outside."

"Why?"

"Because I want to show you something."

"What?"

"Take a look, and find out."

Frowning, Willows went over to the window and peered outside. Down on the street, a pair of cyclists sped past, tyres whining on the wet asphalt, the bikes ticking along like over-wound clocks. Willows looked up through the rain at the dark roof of the building across the street where, three days earlier, the sniper had crouched and fired.

"Look to your left," Parker instructed.

Willows' stomach muscles contracted involuntarily as he leaned out the window and into the path of the bullet that had struck Miriam Okahashi. At the far end of the block a rect-angle of neon hung high above the sidewalk, the light stain-ing the concrete red and green. Because of the rain and the distance, Willows couldn't make out the words on the sign. He withdrew his head, shut and locked the window, and drew the curtain.

"You see the sign?" said Parker.

"What about it?"

"It's a deli. Remember the roast beef sandwich and the container of coleslaw left in the collection booth in the parking lot where Tate and the others were killed?"

"Yes, of course."

"Well, that deli is where the killer bought his meal."

Willows went over to the black leather chesterfield and sat down. The sound of the Muzak in the outer office came faintly through the connecting door. He tried without success to block out an impossibly syrupy arrangement of a tune he recognized but couldn't quite place. "Tell me more," he said at last.

Parker leaned against the desk with her hands in the pockets of the burgundy parka. "Farley Spears and I went over to the deli Friday afternoon, to buy a round of coffee for the forensics team. There was a sign inside pushing a roast beef sandwich and coleslaw combo for the lunch-hour crowd. The sign was what got me thinking. Then I noticed that the guy behind the counter had unusually small hands. And I remembered what George Franklin said at Atkinson's funeral."

"That Goldstein thought the prints on the coleslaw container might have been made by a woman, or someone with small hands."

"Right," said Parker. "The guy behind the counter turned out to be the owner. His name is Carl Heinzman. He and his wife, Gerta, run the place. They don't have any employees, there's just the two of them."

"You told them you were investigating a homicide, and asked them if they'd mind coming downtown."

"They were Austrian. Very cooperative."

"And you found out that Carl Heinzman's prints matched the ones on the coleslaw container."

"Clever you," said Parker. But she'd been the clever one, and they both knew it.

"Did Heinzman remember the sale? Was he able to give you a description?"

"No, but I didn't expect him to. That wasn't the point."

Willows gave her a blank look.

"I checked the yellow pages," said Parker. "There are more than a hundred delicatessens located within the city limits. What do you think the odds are that the killer just happened to pick one located in the same block as his next victim?"

"What are you getting at?" said Willows.

"I'm saying the food in the parking lot was left there on purpose. That the killer deliberately handed us a clue to the identity of his next victim."

Willows stared at her for a moment, and then shook his head in disbelief. "You've got to be kidding. It's crazy. Why would he do something so stupid?"

"Not stupid, risky. But it was a calculated risk. He knew exactly what he was doing." Parker hesitated a moment and then said, "I went right through the master list of all the members of the singles club. Miriam Okahashi is the only one who lived or worked within a ten-block radius of the deli."

Willows still wasn't convinced. "The way I see it, the killer was checking out Okahashi's routine. Or, more likely, he was casing the brick building across the street, making sure he didn't have to worry about a security guard. It was late at night. He saw the deli and decided to grab something to eat, knowing he might have a long wait at the parking lot. But Tate and Moore and Foster left the bar earlier than he'd expected, and he didn't have time to finish his snack." Willows shrugged. "Or maybe he lives or works in the vicinity. Dropped down to the deli for a bite to eat and Okahashi happened to wander in. He saw her and recognized her. Followed her back to her office on impulse, decided to add her to his list. Just one of those things, a coincidence."

"You like coincidences?" said Parker. "Try this one. The day after Phasia Palinkas was shot, we found that the bullet that killed her came from the sporting goods store right across the street from where she dropped."

"Culver's," said Willows.

"Remember the meeting in Bradley's office, when Atkinson said something about the sniper rubbing our faces in it?"

"Yeah, sure."

"Same message, Jack. If we'd known where they'd come from, the two spent cartridges left in the gas station when Alice Palm was shot would've led us straight to Phasia Palinkas."

Willows nodded, thinking back. He recalled with almost preternatural clarity the two gleaming brass shells standing side by side on the counter of the abandoned gas station. He remembered the ribbons of light sifting through the gaps in the wooden hoarding, the brittle, oddly satisfying crunch of broken glass beneath his feet. He saw the rain pounding down, striking white sparks on the asphalt, the bus stranded in the middle of the intersection, windows ablaze with light.

Alice Palm, all in a heap.

"Pink earmuffs."

"What?" said Parker.

"You've made a tenuous connection between Alice Palm and Phasia Palinkas, the three guys who were shot in the parking lot, and Miriam Okahashi. But what about all the rest of the junk we've picked up all over the city? What about, for example, the pink earmuffs left on the sidewalk next to Phasia Palinkas' body?"

"I don't know. I've tried to tie them in, and I can't. Maybe they were tossed in just to confuse us."

Willows smiled. "A pink herring."

"Something like that. There was also the ashtray full of cigarettes in the stolen Mercedes."

"The cigarettes nobody smoked," Willows pointed out.

"Andy Patterson was the next victim. There's a tobacconists right around the corner from the stand where he usually cooped. Why are you looking at me like that?"

"I always wondered how you spent your time when you weren't working," said Willows. "Now I know."

"Patterson used to drop in almost every night, buy a pack of cigarettes or a soft drink. There's a sign in the window advertising the same brand of cigarettes we found in the Mercedes. It could be another coincidence, but somehow I doubt it."

"How do you explain the high-heeled shoe we found on Jervis Street the night Andy Patterson was killed?"

"Just before they were shot, Fraser, Moore and Tate had been drinking at the Rose and Thistle, right?"

Willows didn't respond. He just sat there, waiting for Parker to continue.

"The thing is," said Parker, "that until about a year ago, the Rose and Thistle was called the White Slipper."

"The White Slipper?" If Willows was surprised, he managed not to show it.

"The bartender's only worked there six months, but he told me he understood the business had changed hands a year ago. I talked to the new owner. He said that when he bought the place, it needed a new image. One of the first things he did was change the name."

"And you asked him what the bar was called when he bought it?"

168

"I asked him a lot of things. He happened to mention that the bar used to be called the White Slipper. It just flowed out of the conversation. I got lucky."

"You figure out the Beefeater and the Schweppes bottles, the empty glass and the slice of lime?"

"It's the gin," said Parker.

Outside, Willows stood patiently in the rain while Parker fumbled with her keys. Finally she opened her door and reached across to let him in. The engine started on the first try. She turned on the heater. It growled asthmatically, and a cold damp wind blew across Willows' knees. He wiped condensation from the windshield with the palm of his hand. Parker turned on the lights and released the emergency brake. She put the car in gear and they accelerated away from the curb.

They were on Broadway, heading east through the rain. Because of the lateness of the hour, traffic was fairly light. Parker moved into the centre lane and slowed to turn left on Burrard. They drove down the undulating slope and made a right on Fourth, just catching the yellow. The heater was working now, and the interior of the little car was snug and warm.

At Fir, the light was green. They took the intersection at speed, bumping over a set of railway tracks, passing swiftly through the dense black shadows cast by the massive bulk of the Granville Street bridge. They hit another green at Hemlock, and Willows braced himself as the Volkswagen powered through the corner. Then they were on the glistening black straightway of Sixth Avenue, accelerating past the mass of condominiums huddled along the south shore of False Creek. It was raining harder now, the rain blistering the pavement and frothing in the gutters.

The light at Sixth and Cambie was red. A plugged drain had flooded the intersection. Visibility was less than a block. The windshield wipers struggled with little effect as the hammering on the car's convex roof gradually rose to a thunderous roar. It was deafening, like being inside a tin drum. Willows looked out of the side window and saw that the car was immersed in water right up to the running board. Finally the light changed. They pushed cautiously through the intersection and made the left turn up on to the high ground of the Cambie Street bridge, past the Expo 86 site and the sixty-thousand-seat domed stadium that someone had once described as looking like a huge marshmallow in bondage.

At the north end of the bridge, Parker swung right on to Beatty. Willows rolled down his window a couple of inches and filled his lungs with the cold night air. "Tell me," he said, "why you decided to focus on the gin, instead of the tonic water or the empty glass, the slice of lime."

"Process of elimination," said Parker. "All the other stuff is local, available all over the city. But the Beefeater is one of only two imported brands of gin. All the others are either distilled here or back east, under licence to the parent company."

Willows nodded, not taking his eyes from the road. They were travelling at a steady thirty-five miles an hour and had sailed through three yellow lights in a row.

"Discounting the bootleggers," Parker continued, "every drop of hard liquor in the city is sold through the Liquor Control Board. There are twenty-one retail outlets, including one next to the central warehouse at 238 East Hastings. All imported liquor passes through the warehouse before it's trucked out to the various stores."

There was a large brown envelope lying on the back seat. Parker reached behind her and picked it up, handed it to Willows. The envelope contained seventeen glossy black and white photographs, each measuring eight by ten inches. The top photograph was a closeup of a man Willows judged to be in his early forties. Willows switched on the inside light, and studied the picture carefully. The man's face was heavily lined. He was balding, and his eyes were such a pale grey that Willows was sure they must be blue.

"That's Morris Cunningham," said Parker. "He's a clerk at the warehouse. He's forty-six years old, twice married and twice divorced. He has three children, two by the first marriage and one by the second. His wives have custody. He lives alone in an apartment in the Mount Pleasant district. For the past three weeks he's been on holiday, visiting a brother in Calgary. He goes back to work at eight o'clock tomorrow morning. And

170

there's something about him I think you might find sort of interesting."

"What's that?" said Willows.

"He's a member of the West Coast Singles Club."

Willows turned to the next picture. "Who's this?"

"Clark Wallace, the warehouse manager. All the other pictures are of LCB employees who are scheduled to work at the warehouse or store during the next two weeks."

Willows sifted quickly through the photographs. "Where'd you get these?" he asked.

"LCB security."

"You tell them why you wanted them?"

"No," said Parker.

They were on Powell now, driving east through the unrelenting rain, the clatter of the exhaust beating back at them from the million and one bricks in the gently curving, block-long wall of the BC Sugar refinery. Willows looked at his watch. Midnight had long since come and gone.

Parker slowed, and turned left on Heatley. The car bumped over three parallel sets of railway tracks, feeder lines for the area's many warehouses. The road was narrow, steeply-cambered, ill-lit. Parker switched on the Volkswagen's high beams. They started up a gentle incline. The tracks were on their right, running alongside the road. On their left was a ten-foot-high steel mesh fence topped with barbed wire. Beyond the fence, only blackness. They drove in silence for several minutes. The road levelled out. Parker braked, went into lower gear, and then turned sharply to the left, easing the car through a ragged gap in the fence.

They moved slowly across a span of uneven ground that was strewn with jagged chunks of concrete, abstract tangles of rusty iron pipe. Parker abruptly spun the Volkswagen in a tight half-circle and stopped in the lee of a huge stack of creosote-blacked wooden beams.

Less than twenty feet away, the rust-red prow of a deep-sea freighter loomed high above them. Visibility was so poor that Willows couldn't make out the stern of the vessel, or see the flag she was flying.

"That's the *Seaspray*," said Parker. "She's British registered and she's full of British booze."

"Including a consignment of Beefeaters?"

Parker nodded. "According to the manifest, she's scheduled to start off-loading tomorrow morning at six o'clock sharp. The first truckload is due at the warehouse at eight."

"Who else have you told about this?"

"Nobody. There's two of us and only one of him, right?"

Parker leaned across Willows and flipped open the glove compartment, took out two plastic glasses and a mickey of Cutty Sark identical to the one he'd given her on the night that Fraser, Tate and Moore were murdered. Willows held the glasses while she unscrewed the metal cap.

"I want to bring Franklin in on it," said Willows as Parker poured the Scotch.

"Is that smart, considering the shape he's in?"

"He deserves to be there."

"Then here's to the three of us," said Parker. They touched glasses, drank.

Willows felt the whisky percolating warmly down. The rain looked as if it would never stop, but tomorrow was a brand-new day.

He was looking forward to it.

XX

THE SNIPER LEANED against the curved aluminium railing that enclosed his diminutive balcony. A fitful and capricious wind tugged at his shirt, and at the purple leaves of a Japanese plum tree down on the street. Rain plastered his hair to his scalp and ran into his eyes. He wiped his face with the back of his hand and then peered at the luminous dial of his watch. It was late, almost one o'clock in the morning. He took a last, lingering look down at the drenched and empty streets and then went back inside his apartment and slid the plate-glass door shut behind him.

The apartment had lost much of its charm since he had moved in, only twenty-six days ago. The polished hardwood floors now had a dull, glazed look. Dustballs prospered in the corners. A thin film of oily black dust had settled on the window-ledge and on top of the refrigerator. On the kitchen sink a fat wedge of cheddar cheese lay mouldering, slowly changing from orange to green. The sniper's sleeping bag, fetid and crumpled, lay on the floor surrounded by a wreath of used Kleenex. The once immaculate white walls were covered with the maudlin, disjointed messages he had written to the world during his bouts of drunkenness: the words small and cramped, stumbling over each other, scrawled in Chinese Red lipstick.

A chrome-plated gooseneck lamp cast a small pool of light on the pine work table, but otherwise the apartment was deep in shadow. The sniper stood with his back to the plate-glass door, watching indifferently as a puddle of rainwater collected at his feet. After a few minutes he kicked off his shoes and began to undress, letting his clothes fall where they may. When he was naked, he sat down at the pine table and lit a cigarette, dropping the match negligently on the floor. To his right the rifle lay diagonally across the table, the dark blue metal of the barrel and action gleaming coldly.

The sniper smoked most of his cigarette and then picked up a packet of Kodak cleaning tissue and a small plastic bottle of cleaning fluid. He shook a few drops of the fluid on one of the flimsy tissues, then went to work on the rear lens of the rifle's telescopic sight. As he polished the glass, his thoughts turned once again to Morris Cunningham. The LCB worker had been given a number, and his number was the number nine. The sniper's intention had been to kill four of them at the most, five if it seemed necessary to bump off Foster. But he hadn't planned to kill Tate and Moore, too. Especially not Moore, who hadn't even been a member of the club. Funny how it all slipped away, got out of control. Soon he'd be into uncharted territory, the land of double digits.

What had happened, exactly? How did the situation get so completely out of control? The sniper smiled a wan smile. The answer to his question was right there in front of him, he was holding it in the palms of his hands.

It was power. The incredible sense of limitless power that flowed through him when he cradled the Winchester in his arms and squinted through the Lyman's crosshairs right into the heart of a life.

He tossed the dirty Kodak tissue to the floor, and idly scratched his stomach. It was ten minutes past one. He calculated that it would take him two or three more minutes at most to finish cleaning the scope, only a few more minutes to load the rifle's spare magazines. Add five minutes to strip, clean, reassemble and load the .45 automatic. Half an hour to iron the dress and lay out the rest of his clothes.

When his preparations were complete, he'd take a shower. As always, he would stand rigid and unmoving beneath the coarse jets of scalding water until his neck and chest and shoulders turned red as blood, and he could no longer bear the pain.

Then he'd towel himself off, crawl into the sleeping bag and cry himself to sleep.

Dream of death, and resurrection.

174

XXI

IN ALL DIRECTIONS, as far as the eye could see, the lowering sky was a heavy, leaden grey. It had rained all night, it was raining now, and it was beginning to seem to Willows as if it would rain for ever.

Willows, protected from view if not the weather, was crouched behind the waist-high parapet on the gently sloping roof of the building directly across Hastings Street from the LCB warehouse and liquor store complex. Parker was perched on the roof of the adjoining building, armed with her service revolver and a pair of Zeiss 7X50 binoculars. She'd spotted Morris Cunningham the moment he'd pulled his rusty Chevrolet into the employees' parking lot. Willows had covered Cunningham with his Remington Model 870 Police slug Gun until the unwitting clerk had sauntered into the building, then cradled the heavy gun in his lap and picked up his walkie-talkie.

"Claire?"

"What is it?" Transmitted through the tiny speaker, Parker's voice sounded thin and fragile, crackling not so much with static as with tension.

"Just running an equipment check," said Willows casually. "You remember to put on that high-fashion vest I gave you?"

"And my gumboots. But they leak."

A trickle of cold water ran down Willows' spine, washing away his grin. He adjusted a fold in his poncho and wondered, not for the first time, what the hell had happened to Detective George Franklin.

Franklin was late. And he was so upset with himself that he failed to notice the plump middle-aged native Indian woman sitting in the shadows of the disused loading dock on the far side of the lane.

175

Jenny was a Haida, from the Queen Charlottes. She'd spent the night on the loading dock, nestled snugly in the arms of an unemployed logger named Walt, in a wooden packing crate full of fat white styrofoam worms. They had slept late, waking at nine-thirty, and had killed the next half-hour smoking Walt's hand-rolled cigarettes. At a few minutes to ten, Walt had scuttled across the lane and into a narrow gap between two of the buildings that faced on Hastings. The liquor store opened at ten sharp, and Walt was on his way over to buy a bottle of breakfast.

At two minutes after ten, Franklin appeared in the lane. He was obviously distraught. Jenny watched, fascinated, as he jumped three times in quick succession and then caught the bottom rung of the ladder that Willows had climbed at dawn that morning.

Franklin was winded and gasping for breath when he reached the top of the ladder. He had one leg over the parapet when his sleeve caught on an iron retaining bolt. Cursing softly, he tried to jerk free.

Parker was watching the entrance to the liquor store through her Zeiss binoculars. Willows was busy scanning the roofs of the surrounding buildings. The thin sound of cloth tearing came faintly to him through the rain. He turned around, and then stood up. His walkie-talkie fell unnoticed from his lap into a shallow puddle that had formed in a slight depression in the tar-and-gravel roof. The walkie bounced once and screamed dementedly, making a noise like a dentist's drill.

Franklin scrutinized Willows' face. He watched the flesh rearrange itself to accommodate a tightening of the mouth, noted the distinct loss of warmth around the eyes. Franklin lifted his leg, flashing his new panties, and started back down the ladder. He saw Willows' thumb jab at the safety-catch of the Remington as the barrel of the gun came up and began to swing towards him in a short, smooth arc. The Winchester was slung uselessly over his shoulder. He reached under the white dress and yanked his automatic from the holster strapped to his thigh. Rain fell into his eyes. The heels of his shoes kept catching on the iron rungs. His heart thudded in his chest. Somewhere off to his left he heard the sharp crack of a pistol shot.

Parker, firing steadily, saw puffs of pink dust blossom all around Franklin as her bullets ricocheted off the brick wall of the building. She emptied her revolver and began to reload.

Willows risked a quick look over the parapet. A bullet howled past his face. He ducked back, then pointed the Remington blindly down the side of the building and fired as fast as he could work the slide action.

Iron hummed, sparks flew. Franklin screamed. He let go of the ladder, dropped ten feet and rolled. Slugs cratered the pavement inches away from him as he climbed to his feet. There was a movement off to his right, and he pointed the automatic and fired twice. Jenny fell back into the packing crate, vanishing in a welter of blood.

Franklin began to hobble down the alley. The fall had broken the stiletto heels on both shoes. A slug from the riot gun smacked into a garbage bin and thrummed into the distance, sounding like a single note plucked from a giant harp. Another shot grazed his skull, knocking his wig askew and filling his right ear with blood. He heard the high, urgent wail of a dozen converging sirens. He turned and fired repeatedly at Willows, now halfway down the ladder. Willows braced himself and aimed the riot gun at Franklin.

Franklin hitched up his dress and ran. He hit Walt hard, knocking the wind from his lungs and the brown paper bag out of his hands. A five-dollar bill splintered on the asphalt. Franklin grabbed Walt by his throat and spun him around, using him as a shield. There was a padlocked door only a few feet behind them. Franklin managed to hit the lock with his second shot. He kicked the door open and dragged Walt backwards. Walt scratched at his arm, whimpered like a puppy. Franklin slapped him lightly on the side of the head with the .45. Walt stopped struggling.

Willows was less than thirty feet away, running full-tilt through the rain. Franklin, standing in the doorway, steadied himself against the jamb and took careful aim. Parker stepped around the corner and into his line of fire. The hood of her poncho had fallen back and her face, framed by her hair, was a pale, delicate oval. She was less than an arm's length away. Franklin moved the blade front sight of the automatic across her dark green eyes, the scattering of freckles across the bridge of her nose, her tightly compressed lips, back up to her eyelashes, spiky with rain. His finger curled around the trigger, tightened imperceptibly.

Click.

Parker's eyes glittered feverishly. Time arched its back and showed its teeth. Franklin slammed shut the door.

Willows was clutching her arm, squeezing too hard, glaring at her. "Why the hell didn't you stay up on the roof!"

"Don't you shout at me!" Parker screamed. She wrenched free her arm, glaring at Willows.

Willows tore off his poncho, stuffed shells into the Remington. A cop raced down the alley towards them on his Harley, lights flashing, siren wailing maniacally. Willows heard a clunk as the cop geared down, using the transmission as a brake. The fourteen-thousand-dollar motorcycle fishtailed wildly and then dipped and went over on its side, danced across the lane in a shower of glass and metal and plastic fragments. The cop jumped clear of his bike. He landed on his back and skipped through the puddles like a stone, his Marushi crash helmet trailing a dull white smear on the asphalt.

Willows used the barrel of the Remington gingerly to push open the warehouse door.

"Stay here," he said. "Cover me."

"To hell with you," said Parker. She was right behind Willows as he slipped into the building. The motorcycle cop yelled something. Parker kicked the door shut.

The interior of the building was vast, dimly lit, and perfectly silent. A wide central aisle bisected the floor area. To the left there was row upon row of high steel shelves crammed with cardboard boxes roughly the size and shape of a coffin. Off to the right there was a long conveyor-belt and several large pieces of oddly shaped machinery, including something that looked to Parker like a huge mixmaster.

At the far end of the aisle a cluster of alabaster men and alabaster women stood naked and motionless, caught in a dim circle of light. Like everything else in the building, the figures were covered in a thick layer of fine white dust.

Mannequins. It was a mannequin factory. The creatures were seven feet tall, very thin, with smooth androgynous bodies and wedge-shaped faces that were featureless except for their outsized, brightly-coloured glass eyes.

To Franklin, it seemed that the eyes were gazing coldly and critically down at him, following his every move. He reached out to touch one of the mannequins. Dust sloughed away like a corrupt outer layer of skin.

Walt sneezed.

Franklin heard the door slam shut, heard Willows throw the bolt. He eased a little deeper into the shadows, kicking up small white clouds of dust with every shuffling step he took. He inserted a fresh clip into the automatic, tickled Walt's ear with the barrel.

"What's your name?"

"Walt."

Franklin pressed the barrel against Walt's cheek. "Take a deep breath, Walt, and then scream just as long and loud as you can."

Walt made a croaking sound.

"Louder," said Franklin, and tapped Walt on the bridge of his puffy alcoholic's nose.

Walt screamed.

"Much louder," said Franklin, screwing the barrel of the automatic into Walt's eye.

Walt screamed again, getting off a good one.

"See what you can do when you really try?" said Franklin, patting him on the shoulder.

Willows and Parker had taken cover on the left side of the aisle, behind the first row of steel shelves. The sound of Walt's screams came to them clearly. "He's up at the far end of the building," Willows said to Parker. "I'm going to cut over to the other side, stay behind the machinery and try to outflank him. Force him down to this end. You wait right here. When you're sure of him, take him out."

Parker nodded. She swung out the cylinder of her .38 and checked the load.

"No speeches," said Willows, wanting to make sure there was no doubt in Parker's mind. "Don't say a word to him. Just shoot."

Willows was halfway down the aisle when Franklin started throwing the eyes. The first handful fell short, hitting the concrete floor and bouncing high in the air. Willows dropped and rolled, scrambled behind one of the massive wooden posts that supported the warehouse's roof structure. Dozens more of the eyes clattered on the cement, bounced off the machinery and steel shelves, drummed hollowly on the coffin-shaped cardboard boxes. Willows watched with a dreadful fascination as one of the eyes rolled through the dust and came to rest less than a foot away from him. The eye was exactly the same shade of blue that Dave Atkinson's eyes had been. Willows tightened his grip on the Remington.

Something rumbled softly in the aisle. Willows looked up and saw a handcart speeding towards him, crammed with mannequins in poses that were at the same time both coquettish and grotesque. As the mass of ivory-smooth bodies swayed and shifted in a stiff, self-conscious little dance, clouds of fine white dust boiled up in the wake of the cart. Willows jumped to his feet and peered uncertainly into the milky gloom, caught a glimpse of colour somewhere behind the confused tangle of limbs. He stepped into the aisle and fired the Remington five times in half as many seconds. Heads exploded, bodies were chopped in half, arms and legs shattered. The handcart slowed, and then stopped. Willows hop-scotched through the wreckage. A man lay on his back on the floor. He was covered in dust, as white as a ghost.

Jenny's friend, Walt.

Willows still had the Remington pointed at him when George Franklin stepped casually out from between two rows of shelves and fired from the hip, hitting Willows right in the ten ring. Willows staggered backwards. His hands clenched and unclenched spasmodically. He dropped the Remington. His knees buckled and he started to fall. Franklin shot him a second time, hitting him in the side.

Standing in the classic shooter's stance, her body turned slightly away from the target, legs spread wide and her weapon in a two-handed grip, Parker fired six times at a range of less than twenty feet and missed with all six shots.

Franklin stared at her, his eyes flat and incurious, devoid of life, cold as glass. He smiled at her, and worked the bolt of the Winchester.

Parker willed herself to move, to step back into the deeper shadows between the rows of shelves. She flipped open the cylinder of the revolver, ejected the spent shells and began to reload.

Franklin's attention was deflected by Walt, who was trying to get to his feet. He waited until Walt was on his hands and knees and then, still smiling, shot him through the head.

Parker risked a quick look into the aisle. Franklin waved a plaster forearm at her. He'd tied a square of white cloth torn from his dress to the stump of the arm. Parker forced herself to keep her eyes on him, not to glance down at Willows.

"Is it too late to give up?" said Franklin.

"Better late than never," said Parker. Her voice surprised her. It was weak, shaky. She wondered if she was in shock. She pointed her revolver at Franklin. He skipped back behind a row of shelves.

Parker sat down in the dust. She rested her gun on her thigh and scrubbed her face with her hands. She knew she should keep Franklin talking, because as long as he kept talking, she'd know where he was. But he was a cop, too. Wouldn't he follow the same strategy? And if he did, who had the advantage?

"You remember my partner," said Franklin. "You remember Atkinson?"

"Of course," said Parker. She picked up the .38. It might have been nerves, or an acoustical quirk, but Franklin sounded closer. She stood up.

"He was a real charmer, wouldn't you agree?"

"I wouldn't know," said Parker.

"You went to bed with him, didn't you?"

"What?"

"Come on Claire. Everybody went to bed with Dave, the women couldn't keep their hands off him." Franklin laughed harshly. "Why, he was even sleeping with my wife!"

It wasn't the acoustics, and it wasn't her nerves. Franklin was moving in on her, inching closer with every word he spoke. Crouching, staying low, Parker backed away from the aisle. A

181

hand suddenly slapped at her face, stiff fingers clawing at her eyes. Twisting down and away, she thrust out the revolver and pulled the trigger. The hand disintegrated in a shower of plaster dust. Parker choked back a scream.

"You ever meet my wife?" said Franklin.

"No."

"You sure about that?"

"Yes, of course."

"Just asking," said Franklin mildly. "You mind if I smoke?"

"Help yourself."

"Thank you," said Franklin.

Parker heard the rasp of a match, Franklin exhaling noisily. She knew he had to be very close, that he was waiting for her to panic and bolt into the open.

"Dorothy is forty-three years old and maybe thirty pounds overweight," said Franklin. "What was it about her that Dave found so attractive? I couldn't figure it out, but finally I did. He was sticking it into me at the same time as he was screwing my wife, and that's what really gave him a kick."

"How did you find out about it?" said Parker.

"I'm a detective. It was easy. She confessed."

Parker had a sudden, chilling thought. "Where is Dorothy now, George?"

"Probably stretched out on the chesterfield, watching the soaps." A slight pause. "It was Dave I was after, not her. My only problem was how to knock him off without getting caught. I gave it a lot of thought, Claire. Finally I figured, what better way than in the middle of a homicide investigation?"

"Except it wasn't the middle," said Parker. "It was only the beginning."

"Hey," said Franklin, "maybe I got carried away a little, but don't be so quick to judge. Wait'll you try being God sometime, you'll soon see how hard it is to stop."

Willows lay flat on his back in the rubble, his head cradled between a pair of hard, cold breasts. Dust had settled in his nostrils and the corners of his eyes. He concentrated on Franklin's voice, which seemed garbled, an octave too low, like a tape recording run at the wrong speed. He saw Franklin take another tiny, mincing, cautious step towards Parker. Franklin was only a few feet away but he was too busy hunting Parker to pay any attention to Willows.

Despite the considerable protection afforded by the multiple layers of DuPont Kevlar in Willows' bulletproof vest, the first shot from the .460 Magnum had hit him with so much force that he'd been paralysed by the shock of impact.

Now he was drowning in pain.

Pain flowed in hot, undulating waves from high up in his chest, in the area of his heart. Another kind of pain, sharper and less constant, radiated from his right side. He lifted his head an inch, looking for the Remington. The broken ends of his ribs grated together so loudly that he was sure Franklin must hear them. He repressed a groan, and raised his head another fraction of an inch. The Remington was lying on the floor within easy reach, as if someone had placed it there. Franklin took another mincing step down the aisle. Willows swallowed noisily. The whining in his ears faded away, and he could suddenly understand what Franklin was saying.

". . . not that it was easy, Claire. There were a million details to work out. Where to do it. How to do it. When to do it. Not who to do it to, though." Franklin's giggle was high-pitched, girlish. "That's because I always picked the names at random. You know why? Because it was fairer that way, and I wanted to be fair." A pause. "Are you listening to me, Claire?"

"I'm listening," said Parker.

"The best part, the part I enjoyed the most, was figuring out what kind of junk to leave behind for that overdressed bloodhound Goldstein to chew on, worry over. It gave me a kick, watching Goldstein waste his time."

"I'll bet," said Parker, hardly aware of what she was saying. She could hear the rasp of Franklin's breathing, smell the smoke from his cigarette, almost hear him thinking. Her heart hammered in her chest. She was soaked in sweat, exhausted, limp. She was going to have to do something every soon, take the initiative before Franklin decided to pounce.

"I knew Bradley'd have to stick me behind a desk after Dave got shot," Franklin continued, "but I could hardly believe my luck when he made me assistant liaison officer, dumped me right in the middle of the whole fucking investigation." Another fit of giggling. "From then on, I always knew exactly what everybody was up to, right down to the last detail. It was perfect." Franklin's voice hardened. "At least, it was perfect until you and Jack decided to set up an ambush without telling anybody about it."

"We tried to call you. You weren't at the office. Nobody answered at your home number."

"Oh well," said Franklin, "the main thing is that I eventually got here." Another fit of giggling. "Better late than never."

Willows gritted his teeth. He pushed himself to a sitting position, forced himself to his feet.

Franklin turned, his face slack with amazement. At the same moment, Parker stepped into the aisle and began shooting. She was so close to Franklin that the muzzle blast from her .38 charred and blackened the bodice of his white dress, and the revolver and her hands and wrists turned red with his blood.

Franklin gave Parker a stern, disapproving look. He opened his mouth, licked his lips. Parker reached out and took the Winchester away from him. Their eyes locked. Franklin swayed, and then fell back, arms akimbo. He hit the concrete and dust flew up all around him. He shuddered, and was still. Examining the photographs the next morning, Mel Dutton would marvel at the way the dust that was everywhere had been displaced by Franklin's falling body, pushed back so it formed a cleared space exactly the same shape but slightly larger than his corpse.

Willows limped over, clutching his side. Together, he and Parker knelt beside Franklin.

Franklin's eyes dropped to Willows' chest, the ragged, gaping hole in his jacket and, beneath, the finely woven fabric of the Kevlar vest.

"Clothes make the man, eh, Jack?"

"Looks to me as if we both dressed for the occasion," said Willows.

Franklin gave Willows a sad and empty smile, teeth flashing red with lipstick and blood. He tugged weakly at the tattered hem of his dress. The dark leather of the automatic's holster gleamed against the pale, loose flesh of his thigh. Parker saw that he was wearing panties and that he'd shaved his legs. He mewed like a gull, his fingers plucking feebly at the hem. Was it possible he was embarrassed? Parker pulled the dress down past his knees.

"Sweet thing," croaked Franklin.

"I'm going for an ambulance," said Parker.

Franklin was sweating heavily. The thickly applied makeup on his face had bubbled and ruptured, flowed in thick rivulets down his sunken, stubbled cheeks. He blinked up at Willows and said, "Questions, Jack?"

"Why the singles club?"

"Had to start somewhere, didn't I? It was either that or the phone book."

"Is that where you first met your wife, at the club?"

"Yeah, right. After I decided to kill Atkinson, I went back. First time in a long time, but nothing had changed. I broke in through a rear door. The keys to the filing cabinets were in McCormick's desk. It wasn't locked . . ." Franklin faded. Willows watched him work to gather his strength. "That was my wife in the Christmas picture I hung on the wall in McCormick's office."

"The picture with the shoes in it. Were you having a little fun with us, George?"

"She's still got those shoes. Tucked away in a plastic bag in the attic. I left one just like them on Jervis when I shot Patterson. Hearts stitched above the arch. Real nice. . . ."

Franklin coughed. A fine red mist hung in the air. Blood from the exit wounds in his back had formed a wide pool beside him, crawled along his left arm and wormed its way between his splayed fingers. "I loved her so much," he said quietly. "I loved her so much and it turned out I didn't know her at all." Sunk deep in sockets of mauve and black, Franklin's eyes were listless and dull, the pupils tiny despite the low light level inside the warehouse. He closed his eyes and then opened them, searching for Willows. He clutched spasmodically at Willows' lapel and said, "Talk to me, Jack. I'm dying."

Willows took Franklin's hand, held it firmly. He was bleeding inside, where Franklin had shot him in the ribs. He felt feverish, giddy, full of laughter and panic.

Afterwards, when they asked him what he'd talked about, he couldn't remember a single word.